[sic]

by

Scott Kelly

ISBN-13: 978-1515124412
ISBN-10: 151512441X

Cover by Greg Poszywak

Also by Scott:

The Blue (2014)
Keep the Ghost (2015)

www.ScottKellyWritesBooks.com

1. A return to Earth

MY PERSONAL SAVIOR IS NAMED DAVID BLOOM, and right now he's falling about ten stories from the top of a water tower. And my stupid stunned mind, all I can think is that he looks great doing it. Arms spread, fingertips extended, face serene—homicide by stage dive. His body returns to the earth below, the fall reducing him to a streak of white and blue cloth, brown hair blown back from closed eyes. Maybe he's smiling. Maybe I just like to think so.

I can't see that well. I'm pretty far away, under the cover of some trees, watching through a gap in the leaves. Was supposed to meet someone here.

A masked figure is rushing down the ladder of the tower, half sliding, spider skittering down a drain. David's executioner. At least five people, including me, have a good reason to kill David. Naturally, we've all been friends for life.

A good hero would chase the killer.

I am not a good hero. I'm not even a good me.

I run to the place where David fell, like I think he's still going to be alive, somehow. Stupid. What I get instead shocks me, makes my legs weak and my breath feel worthless. David is no more. This is his face on a sack of meat and bone, limbs bent and joints snapped. This guy—this guy who showed me the light, now just a coffin's worth of flesh.

Still, though. Face frozen in that calm stare. Still looking as good as he possibly can.

Not saying much.

The wet breeze of an incoming cold front sweeps across the woods, and a swarm of blackbirds rises from the trees. If one white dove carries an average soul to Heaven during a funeral, this is a good start. Every grackle in Texas should be heading to the moon. He was a criminal, a drifter, an egomaniac, and my friend.

David was obsessed with finding out what we really are, what a person amounts to when you strip away all the clutter. This obsession resulted in the invention of a game: We call it 'Eureka.'

There's only one rule. Eureka is played like tag, except when touched, you have to change your life in fifteen minutes. Do something, anything that you weren't planning on doing. The more dramatic your change, the better player you are.

Your goals, relationships, and belongings are the cost of entry. Play long enough and life finally becomes about living, rather than some illusion of progress. No attachment to anything except the value of your own continuously thrilling existence.

I've been in a game of Eureka for the past five years, and I've been forced to make changes. Painful changes. What I've earned, though, is a kind of freedom.

The game never stops. One of the other players could tag me; force me to change my life. Anytime, anywhere. Lets me see the real value of things.

Ideally, without regret. *Ideally.* It's how I lost the girl I love.

I pace back and forth, trying not to look but finding myself unable to resist. Still horrifying. Still a puddle of David's parts.

I realize that, for a variety of reasons—not the least of which being, I'm the only one standing around his corpse—I will be blamed for pushing him off the water tower. That's fine. I have some things to discuss with the police.

I blame the death of David Bloom on the weight of his presence. The dead body is a collapsed star, and the resulting black hole will suck everyone else into David's personal reality. My reality.

I close my eyes and inhale slowly, dreading what comes next. I crouch next to David's corpse and reach a hand into his pocket, trying to avoid all contact with my dead friend's flesh. I can't help nudging him. He shifts limply; a shattered arm bends backward. Sick. I yank the cell phone he carries from his pocket.

The phone works; I dial nine one one. "There's a dead body at the water tower next to the Kingwood High football field." My voice cracks. Putting words to this somehow makes things worse.

The responder rattles off questions, making sure I'm serious. Eventually, she's convinced this is real and I hang up.

The high school football field is a half-mile back, and they're holding our graduation today. My would-be girlfriend, the valedictorian, will be giving her graduation speech. Doesn't matter—she's not talking to me anymore.

I pull a beat up pack of cigarettes from my pocket. They aren't mine, and I don't smoke. One left; I remove it, then take the pack, wipe it on my shirt, and throw it into the grass. A small quotation is scrawled on the paper tube in tiny script. It reads *Hell is other people*. Appropriate. I hold a flame to the end of the nicotine stick until the tip smolders, then place the softly smoking cylinder next to David's body. The cigarette smokes itself: tiny prayer candle to my friend.

How did I let things come this far? The sorrow sets in as my adrenaline drains. I'm going to miss him. I'm truly alone.

A squad car arrives. A Hispanic policeman steps toward me; the way he alternates between jogging and walking makes his excitement evident. I lift my hands above my head to show I'm unarmed and cooperative, then point at David's body. The policeman teeters around the corpse, first crouching nearby, then standing over, and finally touching the cadaver for a pulse.

"I need you to arrest me," I tell him, once he's balanced enough to move forward.

The officer asks me: "Did you kill this boy? Do you know what happened?"

I don't say another word. After a few more unanswered questions, the handcuffs click around my wrists. Hands brush my pockets, my socks. Strange intimacy. I'm loaded into the cruiser.

"What happened out there?" he asks as we drive to the police station.

"Are you the person that decides whether or not I am going to get charged with murder?" I ask instead, ignoring the question.

The cop clears his throat, agitation evident. "No, I'm not. You'll be talking with a detective."

"Then I'll talk to the detective," I say. "Until then, I'm invoking my fifth, or whatever you call it."

"Your right to remain silent," he explains.

"Right, that."

There are dark clouds overhead, and the first drops of rain start falling just as we reach the police station. I try to remind myself that this doesn't matter either way. I've never owned anything, and never will. No good or bad situations, only experiences. Everything matters because nothing matters; I know this because of what David taught me. Because of Eureka. I lean my forehead against the cool glass of the police cruiser window and remember him.

2. David Bloom

Eighth grade

A SWARM OF GRACKLES SHRIEKED in discord from the tall oak behind us. I turned to watch them; blackbirds with iridescent bodies like something born of oil spills. Texas' answer to the raven. When a sudden noise startled the birds, they burst away in a black cloud. All for the slamming of a trailer door—the calamity in Broadway Trailer Park even annoyed the pests.

Just beyond the bus stop, a fat man in a tank top screamed from his doorstep at a neighbor, hurling an empty bottle of beer at her RV. His elderly target stood in her yard, shrieking, brandishing a small garden rake, bulwarked by black garbage bags. The holy mess of our lives: big barking dogs in makeshift fences, beer guts in ripped jeans, and high drama at loud volume.

David and I stood at the road outside the park, watching as we waited for the morning bus to school. His skin shone against low-hanging sun, wisps of curled brown hair wild, accidentally styled by his mom's rough haircuts. Fourteen, two years older than me—tall and lean.

The bus was always late, which always made us late, which highlighted the fact we were from a different part of town than our classmates. In Kingwood, kids' parents drove them to school, usually in something expensive.

When our bus finally rumbled to a stop, David and I let the other four kids from Broadway get in first. The ride was quiet, the morning's chaos having earmarked the day. We peered out our respective windows as the wilderness of the forest around Broadway Trailer Park transformed into the pristine town of Kingwood, with its vaguely Italian cream colored buildings and new football stadium.

The high school and middle school were only a hundred feet apart, sharing bus routes and sports fields. We rolled into the parking lot.

None of us wanted to be here. Hand-me-down sneakers, hungry for free school lunches—no one pretended we belonged, least of all us.

Even after the bus driver cut the engine, none of us moved. We sat together, staring at the floor or the ceiling or our hands—anything but each other. Like we could just hide here until school was over, and not have to go inside.

It took a few minutes, but David was the first to stand. "Come on," he said. "Let's go."

After school, I waited for David near the bus stop. Worst part of my day: no one rode the bus except the kids from Broadway, and so the spot was ripe for ambushes.

A high school boy approached. Trouble. I recognized him as one of the meanest bullies in his grade—my regular after-school problem. Twice my size, at least; a boiled gorilla that stank like ranch corn chips and an unwiped ass.

"Hey, buddy," he said, voice low and slow. "Make any crystal meth today?" He snickered at his own joke.

Bad day to be standing alone. I ignored him, wishing one of us would disappear. Fighting back never got me far with this one; he was too big.

He stepped up, electric-blue shirt and its flipped up collar inches from my face. The line of sweat underneath his flabby chest lined up with my eyes as I stared straight ahead.

My tormenter spun me around and gripped my backpack, holding it so I couldn't run.

"What's that all over your shirt?" he asked, pointing down at the white paint splotches on my black t-shirt. "Even the clothes you steal suck." The observation was cut short as David collided with the bulky boy; he tumbled to the ground, fat face bouncing off the grass.

The bully climbed to his feet, cheeks red, and faced David. They rushed each other. The larger boy stepped forward and kicked, shoving my friend back with his foot. David staggered then lunged, arms swinging in a series of akimbo assaults, fists flailing like a carnival clacker.

It wasn't enough to overcome the superior bulk of our enemy; he pushed past David's fists, ramming a palm into his forehead.

David grabbed the hand and bit in. Blood peaked from under his canines and ran down the bully's fingers. The stunned student tried to pull away, but David clamped down harder, teeth slowly sinking through delicate tissue.

No more pretending: our tyrant hissed in pain, eyes clenched shut. The feel of David's teeth grinding against his bones, the flesh tearing as he jerked away—these were not things he came prepared to feel, and I saw tears at the corners of his eyes.

I panicked, realizing I'd have to stop David again. My shoulder hit his side as I tackled my friend; he released his hold. The bully fell out of reach, but David yanked out of my grip and started kicking at him again and again, aiming for ears and neck and nose. I grabbed his arm and pulled.

Finally, the older boy got up off the ground and limped away— crying as he wrapped the bleeding hand in his shirt.

David wiped the blood from his chin; a droplet fell into the dirt. His hair matted to his forehead where the sweaty hand had pressed against it. Five and a half feet of tightly wound determination.

"C'mon," David said, voice hoarse.

I followed in stunned silence. Only David rebelled—tooth and nail.

A soft knock woke me from my sleep. I twisted in my cot, pulling back the bed sheets I hung as curtains. Knuckles rapped against the little plastic porthole; I pressed my face to the window and saw David stood outside. I checked the wristwatch beside my bed: 3 AM.

Only needed jeans and a shirt; on a balmy spring night in South Texas, you didn't need the sun to sweat. I found David perched over a chrome bicycle near the trailer. A bulging backpack hung around his shoulders, and a second bike lay on the ground next to him.

"What's going on?" I asked, vision cloudy.

"My paper route," he said. "I want you to come with me tonight. I've gotta show you something."

"Paper route? Don't you have school?"

"Sleep is a waste, if you think about it."

I pulled up the second bike: a diamond-shaped red frame with shocks and knobby tires. The clamp underneath the seat was stuck; I banged on the padding with my elbow until the saddle lowered into a position I could get my leg over. "And where'd you get this?"

"I borrowed it. C'mon, let's go." David stood as he pushed the pedals, accelerating quickly. I struggled to keep up. My new bike crunched through its gears, metal on metal.

We sped down the freshly paved road leading to Kingwood. No cars; the world was ours. Thick sheets of darkness ruffled my hair and teased my skin. Exhilarated.

A couple miles later, we made a right turn into a proper Kingwood neighborhood. A newer one, the trees still saplings, but laid out in a big figure eight like all the rest. David pulled off to the side, under a street light but away from any houses.

"Check this out," he said, sliding the backpack off his shoulders and digging through it, retrieving a large chart folded into thirds and marked with addresses and instructions. "This is my paper route. They give me a new one every week. The route is stupid, but look: people tell us when they're going on vacation. Know why? They don't want the papers piling up out front, so it won't look like they're gone. But, it says right here how long they'll be gone, and when they'll be back."

"Okay. And?" I got off the seat and stood over the frame, on my toes to keep the aluminum bar from digging into my crotch.

"So, I can break in without getting caught," David said, smiling. Teeth white, practically light sources in their own right. "Some of them are gone for weeks. You just find a good one, in a corner somewhere."

David mounted his bike and pedaled off; he hopped a curb and we pushed through the grass outside a small brick house. Through the yard and right up to the back door—the realization I was about to break the law dawned on me; I got off my bike and stood dumbly, unable to continue.

David turned. "Come on, don't be a wimp. I've been in here a bunch, it's fine."

He fished a key from the backpack and opened the back door. "I used the window the first time," he informed, retrieving a flashlight. "Just took a key from the cabinet after that. C'mon, pull the bikes in, don't want them sitting outside."

A sudden, crushing anxiety forced itself on me. I was about to go in someone else's home, their sanctuary, without their approval. I couldn't move; cold sweat clung to my skin.

"C'mon," David insisted. "Follow me."

I did as he instructed, guiding my bike over the white tiled floor of a clean kitchen. Only a green mop, perched against the refrigerator, stood out of place. It felt *wrong* to be inside this home, with other people's aunts and uncles on the walls leering at me accusingly.

After a few breaths, I regained control of my legs. An upright piano occupied the far corner of the living room, covered with photos and trinkets, keys blanketed with a red cloth. I studied one of the pictures: a middle-aged woman with a short, tidy haircut. Modest makeup, long dress, no jewelry. Very reserved.

"That's Pamela. It's her house; she's divorced, has one kid who grew up. She's an accountant. Come on," David said, motioning toward a hallway leading deeper into the house.

He guided me into the bedroom, flashlight leading the way through the darkness. "It's crazy, you know—being in someone's house is like being in their head. All the stuff in the living room, the stuff other people see, it's about her being this nice mom and accountant. But when you get a little deeper—look, come in here."

He led me to the last room in the house, furthest away from any entrances. A walk-in closet, filled with drab dresses in neutral colors. We pushed our way through the forest of clothes and reached the far corner.

He folded back the dresses to reveal a worn banker's box. Within: books of sheet music, some loose and others bound in tomes. Bach, Chopin, Beethoven. There were photos as well, of Pamela as a young girl all the way into adulthood, seated at a piano in concert halls and private practice rooms. In one, an orchestra sat behind her as she smiled in concentration at the keys. "She used to play. Must have quit; there's junk all over the one in the living room. Tucked it all away in here, you know? She wakes up every morning, and lives in an accountant's house. So—is the box in the closet because she stopped playing piano, or did she stop playing because the box is in the closet?" He picked up the container of Pamela's music. I followed him out to the living room.

"What are you doing?" I asked as he set the cardboard box down on the piano bench.

"Rearranging her priorities," David answered.

"You think that's a good idea? Isn't this wrong? Won't she find out?"

He shrugged. "I won't get caught; I'm not stealing anything."

"It's still wrong!" I exclaimed. "You're trespassing, you're spying —not stealing doesn't make this okay."

"Objection noted," David said. He began to clear away the clutter that sat atop the piano, carefully folding up a picture of Pamela hugging an elderly man. Next, her framed degree in accounting. Then a set of white candles, and finally, the red cloth that covered the instrument.

"How often do you do something like this?" I asked.

"Often," he said simply, putting a music book on the piano's stand and flipping through it. "I just dig around, you know? Not stealing, just curious. She's going to know someone wants her to play piano. Does the home make the person, or does the person make the home? We live in a shithole, and the people there are shit. This house is nice, the lady seems nice, too."

"Aren't you just going to scare the Jesus out of her, when she finds out someone broke into her home?"

David shrugged, smiling as he placed a picture of young Pamela at the piano inside the book of music. "I've been scared before. It's not that bad."

3. You're in luck. I'm the normal one.

Now

M Y HANDLER OPENS THE CAR DOOR; I step out of his cruiser and am surrounded by people in uniforms. Latex gloves shield their skin from me. They untie and strip away my shoes.

"You can keep them," I offer.

The guard grunts and opens a thick metal door, leading me by the arm into the jail itself. My feet are cold against the linoleum; colored lines mark paths for the inmates to walk from one area to the next. Signs explain: red is for meals, black for administration, and blue for court.

The far corner of the jail is a large cell where a group of bored looking men sit. We follow the black line to a sort of doctor's office. The handcuffs release with a rapid series of metallic clicks; I like the sound. A woman grabs my wrist with one hand and fingers with another, pressing them into an ink pad, then onto a sheet of paper next to the words "Jacob Thorke."

Jacob Thorke. My label, but not the description of a person. The prints are the most permanent thing about me.

After this, we walk to a small office inhabited by a sweaty policeman who—judging from the grimace on his face—appears to be in pain. He stands as I enter; easily triple my width, and a foot taller. I'm directed to a chair that faces his, placed so close together, I can't imagine where our legs will go. As we both sit, I feel I'm nearly in his lap—our noses almost touch. This forces eye contact, forces attention. There's no ignoring him.

As he watches me, tortured grunts escape his fat lips and puff hotly against my cheek. "What happened to David Bloom?" he asks.

"Jealousy. Betrayal. Maybe revenge? I'm not sure. Do you have any idea what kind of person David was?"

"I know he was practically homeless. I know he was valedictorian of his class, though that's got a controversy attached to it. I also suspect he was an arsonist, although we never managed to prove it." The detective reaches into a black leather case sitting open at his feet and retrieves a file.

"Arsonist?" News to me.

"I could probably tie him to two separate fires, same time period he did a dozen home invasions. About six years ago. No deaths, though, and not enough evidence for an arrest."

Hearing this is like being punched in the stomach. *David was burning down houses?* I thought we had no secrets.

I give him one word in response: "Interesting."

"You know what happened to David Bloom?" he asks.

"Someone wearing a mask pushed him off the water tower. I got there just in time to see him fall; I don't know who pushed him. I didn't get a good look. I can narrow it down to four people now—his followers. I used to be one of them. But, I have a psychologist, a special advocate for children's something or other. His name is Mr. Aschen, and he counseled David and I. If he were here, I'd happily give you more details about what I suspect happened, and he could corroborate it."

"You said David had 'followers.' He was the leader of what, like a gang or something?"

"More like a cult." If my counselor heard me admit this, he'd celebrate with champagne.

Another groan as my interrogator stands and moves to a small bookshelf lined with yearbooks. "Sadly, I find these to be very handy in my line of work. What year?"

"I'm a senior this year. I'd be graduating...right now."

The most recent yearbook is pulled. "Give me names. Faces. Then we'll talk about your counselor."

Can smell the fresh ink as the pages are peeled open; the laminate squeaks under my fingers. "You're going to love these. You've got records on all of them, I'm sure. Let's see. You'd have a file on this guy," I point at a wiry little nerd with glasses. Under the picture: *Steven Thomas.* "In connection with one landlord of Broadway Park, whom my friend Steven wanted to kill, but settled on having arrested. He's...wrathful."

"*Wrathful?*" the detective asks, a bemused grin forming.

"Like the Old Testament." The pages fan the cop's reeking breath away as they flip. I stop at the baseball team's photo and point at a chubby, egg-shaped kid on the far right. "Kent Gimble. His dad—the aforementioned landlord—tortured us growing up, and molested one of the girls. So there's that file, and also one you've got on Kent for a manslaughter charge you stuck him with. Oh, and the drugs, but the nerdy kid framed him for that. Hell, Kent might be in this jail right now."

The detective grunts as I flip through the pages, stopping on a full-color photo of a young girl. She is vibrant with life like beehives and freshly fallen fruit. She has curled, crimson tinged hair and tan skin, and looks like someone an ancient hero would find bathing in a lake.

"Cameron Merrill. Object of the child molester's desires. Mom was a whore. The wrathful kid and the big kid both have a history of fighting over her. But, she was sleeping with the guy who died—David."

The detective murmurs something, but I'm too excited by the next face staring out of the book. A pale-skinned girl with thick, dark makeup, looking like the reanimated corpse of a homecoming queen. "Emily Maebe. Also screwing David. And me, sometimes. Otherwise, just screwing *with* me. You've got her down for identity theft and grand theft auto. Or at least, you should."

He cracks his knuckles. "And who was this landlord? Kent Gimble's father?"

"You've arrested him at least once before, for molesting Cameron. He tortured all of us—some, more than others. Without him, we wouldn't have any of this. David never would have become who he did, and the others wouldn't have listened to him."

My keeper leans back and runs a hand over his barren scalp. Another pained sigh escapes him; a pack of antacids is torn open and five are eaten.

"You're a screwed up bunch of kids." A grunt is cut short by a hollow laugh. He takes the yearbook away and we lock eyes.

"You're in luck. I'm the normal one," I say, grinning.

"I'll get your counselor, if you tell us everything that happened. Until then, we're going to hold onto you. Within forty-eight hours we will either charge or release you. Think about that."

No way can I ignore it. Guards lead me back to my own private holding tank. I sit on the single concrete bench and lean my head against the wall. I think back to the first thing I can blame for the death of David Bloom. Before Eureka, before any of it, came the problems that forced us to make changes. Problems that still haunt us today.

4. Landlord

Eighth grade

I LIKED TO ROAM AROUND THE WOODS outside of Broadway after school, instead of going home. Anything to stay out of the trailer park, I suppose.

The forest–Kingwood's namesake–bordered a marsh, and the soil always flooded. Only fresh ferns and towering trees sprouted from the earth, and I stepped around both as I wandered through the thicket. Once the trailers were out of sight, it was easy for my imagination to take over and transform the forest into my playground.

A loud metallic snap clapped in my ear. A bird began screeching from the ground behind me–a distress call, same shrill note played on repeat. I followed the sound: one of the iridescent birds, a male grackle, struggled in the dirt. One wing flapped, the other stuck extended; the bird pivoted on the wrecked wing, incapable of understanding its body was broken, or determined to fight anyway.

Its struggles intensified as a chubby, pale young boy approached, air rifle in hand, serious look on his face. The grackle's frantic calls sped in rhythm, sporadic squalling, as a foot lowered on its head.

A muffled pop. The bird fell silent.

Shocked, I watched the landlord's son. Kent was my age, in my grade. But, his dad abused our parents–and us–regularly, so Kent was an outcast twice over, lonely prince of Crap Mountain.

Kind of weird, too. Short blond hair, big head that melted into his squat body. Eyes squinted into angry slits, like the bird wronged him somehow.

I started to back away, hoping to avoid him.

"Hey, Jacob."

No luck.

"Hey," I said. "What are you doing?"

"I have to kill grackles," Kent mumbled.

"Why?"

"Dad says they're keeping people away." My neighbor stared at the still bird below us. "I hate when they don't die fast. Come on, I gotta go get a trash bag."

Kent walked back to the trailer park; I followed.

"I have to kill three grackles a day," he said as we trudged along.

"That sucks."

We stopped at the corner of the Broadway property, at the nicest trailer on the lot. The home of the landlord, hulking and squat, white plastic glistening in the sun.

Kent's dad slept under an awning outside his trailer. Rolls of fat spilled out from the sides of the lawn chair. A sweaty thatch of faded yellow hair gave way to heavy cheeks and thick jowls. Kent's dad looked sad—not mad at all. Just a defeated frown, like he was about to start bawling in his sleep. Like dreaming was torment. Like it hurt to be.

Kent motioned for me to follow him into the trailer; I did so, creeping over the grass and up the steps. I held the door for Kent then closed it gently behind me, relieved to be away from his dad. Kent flipped on the lights, revealing the shining surfaces of a high-quality mobile home, full kitchen and tidy living room. He leaned the air rifle against the wall, then opened a cabinet under the sink.

We were interrupted by a timid knock on the back door. The sound came from the opposite side, away from the slumbering landlord. Kent abandoned his search for a trash bag and crossed the living room, opening the door.

A girl my age stood in the doorway, lips pressed tightly together, stress evident in the lines on her forehead. Cameron's hair was an angry mess of strawberry blonde curls; she held a package of sugar in her hand. The package was half-full, rolled over at the top, and looked ancient and dirty.

"Mom sent me to give your dad this," Cameron said, voice tired. "Hi, Jacob."

"Hey, Cameron," I responded.

"My dad's asleep," Kent said. "You should go before he wakes up."

Cameron nodded, smiling. Her tension released immediately, smooth complexion returning.

A sound came from the opposite end of the trailer: the creaking of a lawn chair, then cursing, a steady low mumble like the idling of a diesel truck. "Go!" Kent said. She turned and hurried away, sugar in hand.

Just as Cameron left, Kent's dad pushed the front door of the trailer open, dark figure forming a silhouette in the sunlight. The steady stream of curses was broken up by three real words: "Who was that?"

"Just Jacob," Kent said, pointing his thumb at me.

Mr. Gimble stepped inside, twisting his body slightly to fit through the door. Beady eyes honed in on me. "No friends over," he declared.

Kent shrugged helplessly.

"I said, no friends over!" Mr. Gimble shouted a moment later. I jumped, shocked by the sudden outburst. Kent pushed the back door open and put a hand behind my back, forcing me through. I didn't argue, hurrying out instead. Kent followed, sighing an apology the moment he stepped outside.

"Goddamnit, Kent!" a voice roared from inside the trailer. The steady stream of curses renewed; I turned to Kent. The color drained from his face.

"What'd you do?" I asked.

My neighbor shrugged, bottom lip trembling, eyes wet. The answer was obvious, the question redundant: he'd done something, somewhere—or maybe nothing, nowhere—and would be punished.

I grabbed Kent's arm. "Come on. Come with me."

He shook his head *no* and brushed my hand away. The door of the trailer opened. Survival instincts kicked in: I ran, leaving Kent to his fate.

I jogged out of the park. Strange, how even the open air made me claustrophobic.

The paths within Broadway were rough gravel; white shale shifting under my feet as I walked. There was a special way you learned to move in the park, always expecting the ground to slide out from under you. No going barefoot. Where the path ended, a slick black road connected Broadway to the rest of Kingwood. The road, property of Kingwood County.

The way was lonely; seldom traveled. A crisp white SUV flew down the street, gleaming in the evening light. *Baby on board.* Child seats and DVD players; leather upholsteries and air conditioning. Nice things for nice people.

5. Eureka

Eighth grade

EVENING, AND THE ADULTS WERE FIGHTING AGAIN. I sat on a slight hill, chin on my knees, between two tall oaks. Enough ivy underneath to keep my shorts from getting dirty. The other five kids who lived in Broadway sat nearby, silent, hiding with me at the tree line. We always listened to the grown ups fight; it let us know what we'd be in for that night.

"She's worthless!" Kent's dad yelled, shoulder hair climbing around the straps of his wife beater. He pointed at the pile of trash bags surrounding David's trailer. "Place looks like hell because of her. That's why the grackles come and cover this place in bird shit—because she dumps garbage on her front steps, like an animal. Everyone else cleans up. She should clean up, too. I'm fed up with it."

Dad stood between the landlord and David's trailer, hands raised, palms open. Apologizing, trying to calm Mr. Gimble down—I couldn't hear him from here, but I'd seen this play out before. David's sick mom could barely leave the trailer, let alone take the trash out. Didn't seem to matter until Kent's dad was drunk enough.

Could almost feel Kent behind me, where I knew he sat. Too awkward to look back. I tore a clump of three-leaf clovers from the ground and twisted the plants in my fingers.

Mr. Gimble's gut looked like the egg from which he was still emerging, and the flesh jiggled as he pivoted, lunging for my dad. Dad stepped back; the landlord tripped in the gravel, landing on his side. The grown man howled, clutching the arm he'd landed on.

Dad took the opportunity to retreat, long legs leading him back to his car. Red-faced and cursing, he shut the door, locked it, and pulled a small bottle from the glove compartment. We watched him unscrew the top and take a drink. He usually drank in the car, especially when he thought I was home. Didn't drive anywhere, just sat there and listened to the radio.

Mr. Gimble staggered to his feet. I got a glimmer of hope as he stumbled back to his trailer—finally, he was inside. We could let our guard down, at least for now.

I stood and wiped the grass from my shorts. Nighttime; had to get home before eight, or I'd get in trouble.

"Gotta go," I said, turning to leave.

"Wait!" David's voice behind me. He walked up, smiling. "What are you about to do?"

All eyes on me. "I'm about to go home and lay down, I guess," I said, unsure, pointing my thumb at my trailer.

"Why?" he asked.

"Because it's time. It's night, that's when Dad wants me back."

David took a step closer, five fingers on his left hand pointing at me to emphasize the point. "We all stay out late. Your dad's getting drunk in his car, Jake. You think he minds? Stay out with us. You always go home; you don't need to."

Suddenly I couldn't swallow; strange wetness in my eyes.

He continued, voice softening: "Sorry, look. I want to try an experiment. I watch you walk back there, seems like every night, while we stay out here and have fun. You don't want to go, right? But it's what you do. You go home at eight, for no real reason—no one is watching us. What if I just...derailed you, right now?"

The others came closer. I felt Emily, Cameron and Steven press in. Only Kent held back.

"What do you mean, derail me?"

David walked closer, enough to touch me. The last bit of sun fell below the trees, and he was shadow-clad. His hand rose into the air, then landed on my shoulder. "Do anything other than going back to your trailer." His voice was stern, commanding.

Everyone watched me as I turned to look at my home. Anywhere but there.

The road out of Kingwood ran to the left of the little white, wheeled box I called home. Further still, the woods I'd grown familiar with. Still further left, my friends. Just a moment ago, these things hadn't been options; all I saw was my trailer. Now, though: "Okay. I'll stay here, then, with you guys."

"Eureka," David said. "How do you feel?"

"A little weird," I answered, walking toward the woods. I got a little thrill—something about disobeying my dad.

"My turn," Steven said. He walked between David and I, six inches shorter with thick glasses. "Let me try."

I stopped, looked at David. He turned to me. "You do it. You're 'it' now. Steven goes—give him fifteen minutes. After he's done, he picks who is next. That's all."

A new game, then. I put my hand on Steven's shoulder. "Tag," I said. With no hesitation, he ran deeper into the woods.

"I want to swim in the creek, come on," he called. Cameron and Emily laughed, jogging after him.

I searched for the moon between the trees. Couldn't find it. Only a single grackle, which rested on a dead limb of cypress that rose over the treetop canopy. I followed my friends.

6. Day one

Eighth grade

ANOTHER DAY. I was exhausted, but happy—didn't get any real sleep the night before; didn't even get in bed until three in the morning. But, it'd been fun. Still had silt between my toes, could feel the sand in my sock.

Now, though, it was back to the real world. I stuck a finger through the cigarette burn in my shirt, sighing. The bus rolled to a stop outside the school. All six of us walked slowly out, packs heavy on our backs, and stood in the parking lot between the middle and high schools.

David soldiered on to the high school alone, saying farewell with a nonchalant wave. I turned to my friends—they looked as exhausted as I felt; purple bruises under bloodshot eyes.

A wet squelch came from Steven's shoe. We made eye contact and both cracked smiles. "You tired?" I asked as we began our walk to class.

"Totally worth it," he said, smile widening. Steven carried his backpack in both arms, as the straps had long since broken. His voice dropped conspiratorially. "Watch this."

My glasses-clad friend crept away from me, toward Kent. He snuck up behind the much larger boy and slapped his free hand down on the back of the landlord's son.

"Tag," Steven said. "You're 'it!'"

Kent spun, lifting his hands to defend himself. When he saw it was only Steven, he relaxed. "We're not playing anymore," he said. "It's school."

"Who says we're not playing?" I asked. "David didn't say the game was over, you know. C'mon, it's not hard. Just take whatever you were about to do, and don't do it. Do something else."

Kent looked around. A few dozen of our classmates stood outside the entrance, near the flag pole. His face turned red; he turned again, looking back at us. Finally, his eyes rested on Steven and the backpack in his arms.

Kent slammed a meaty fist down on the bag. Steven gawked as it hit the ground with a vicious *whomp.*

"Now you're 'it' again," Kent said slowly.

Steven shrugged helplessly. "Great. Good idea, Kent," he murmured, leaning down to pick up his bag. He looked at me and shook his head as the bell rang.

On to class; desperate to stay awake. Teachers seemed to feel sorry for me, probably my clothes—usually wasn't hard to put my head down in a corner desk and let the class go on without me.

So it went. Soon the blessed ringing came; I grabbed my backpack and stepped out the class. I spotted Steven exiting a room a few hundred feet from me—it occurred to me that he was 'it' again. I stood a safe distance away; didn't want to have to play David's new game in front of the entire school.

Steven snuck up behind a girl with strawberry blonde hair: Cameron. He put a hand on her shoulder; she turned. I imagined a single word was exchanged between them.

The moment he lifted his hand away, Cameron gripped the boy by the shoulders and pulled him into her, like she wanted to head-butt the young geek, but no, her lips were pursed and, holy crap, she kissed him. Steven cringed so hard he might be trying to disappear into himself. Instead, their lips met in an angry mash, both parties seemingly terrified by the act, Steven's thick glasses pushed lopsided up on his forehead as Cameron leaned down to meet him.

I heard a gasp; I turned to my right. Kent. He stood with his mouth gaping, face colorless, looking sick.

A coach snatched Cameron's arm in one hand and Steven's in another, dragging them toward the office. Emily noticed their plight and walked to them, dark chocolate hair bouncing with each step.

Cameron reached out with her free hand and gripped Emily's in passing, like they were sharing a note. Not the case, though.

Emily spun and intercepted the coach who held Cameron and Steven. She leapt into the older man, arms clinging to his shoulders, pulling him close, lips extended. The coach, quadruple her size, resisted, pulling away—Emily hung from the big man's neck like jewelry until at last he peeled her off, face four shades of crimson.

The coach laughed, all confusion and disapproving head shakes. He opened his mouth and then closed it, glancing around. Dozens of students in the halls, but no other teachers.

Emily only stood and smiled, hands folded behind her back, studying him.

The adult shook his head, ran a hand over his bald scalp. His mouth opened then closed again; still no words. After a moment, the coach appeared to grow angry, but still had no response. Finally, he continued to pull Steven—who wore the biggest, stupidest smile I'd ever seen—and Cameron to the office.

Emily continued walking, kitten smile on her lips. She approached Kent and me.

I swallowed back cold fear. Was it my turn?

Kent shoved me out of the way, intercepting Emily. "Tag me!" he demanded.

"You just got tagged," Emily noted. "It was lame."

"I didn't do it right."

"You'll get another turn," she said. Then she arched an eyebrow. "You just want to kiss Cameron, don't you?"

"I, well, I just..." The bell rang, freeing Kent from the clumsy justification.

If she wasn't tagging him, then it must be me. I looked pleadingly at Emily, hoping to get this over with. She only shrugged and turned away.

Frustrating. I raced to next period to keep from being late. Class was torture; I couldn't keep my mind off her. She must be waiting to tag me. When the period finally ended, I walked cautiously into the hallway, checked right and left, and...

No Emily. I walked around, looking up and down the halls, but —no Emily. On to the next class. And the next.

I spent the rest of the day anxious for her to appear. Kent and Steven passed by multiple times, and when I asked about her, neither had answers for me.

Finally, last period: English. I stopped in the doorway. Could see from here—my name was written on the whiteboard in red marker. The last in a long list of speakers, the rest of whose names were erased days earlier.

Christ. Book reports. I'd known about this for weeks. In fact, an essay on "The Giver" sat on my bed at home.

A soft hand touched my neck, flesh hot against mine. "Tag." A girl's voice—Emily.

"Nice," I mumbled.

"Fifteen minutes," she said.

I crossed the threshold and sank down in a chair, putting my backpack up on my desk and half hiding behind the bag. Classmates chuckled.

My teacher—a thin lady with a wide, pronounced mouth and formidable front teeth, gnawed her way through roll call. I tried desperately to remember what I'd written, but nothing came.

"Jacob, since you had the good luck of going last, I expect this to be an exemplary report," Mrs. Kerrigan's voice was thick as syrup.

Emily's face smiled out the small window in the classroom door.

Ten minutes to change. What would I normally do at a time like this? Tell the teacher I'm not ready, go back and sit at my desk in shame? But, I'm not ready—can't change that.

I walked to the front of the class, behind the podium. Could feel their eyes on me.

"I read..." I began. Fellow students stared skeptically. I watched them: the Austins, the Baileys, the Coltons. Wasn't friends with any of them. Didn't dislike them, but we were from two different worlds.

So, this is Eureka. Change anything.

"I read a book about a boy who lives in a trailer." Everyone was silent, now. "Every weekend, he puts his dirty clothes in a sack and walks half a mile to the Laundromat. He sits in there for two hours every Saturday morning, wondering what everyone else gets to do when they wake up. Then he puts on the clothes he washed–his dad's, really, since he outgrew his this year and hasn't got any new ones–and wears them to school, because even the teachers will say something if he wears dirty clothes and stinks. People make fun of him for what he wears, but he knows they don't even have to wash their own clothes, and that's not fair. Everyone treats him like he chooses to dress that way, even though he doesn't."

Some kids in the back glanced at one another, chuckling. Red heat climbed my cheeks. "At the end of the book, he, um, he..." My voice cracked; more chuckling. If I talked anymore, I knew it wouldn't come out clear. "I didn't finish reading the book," I mumbled.

I hoped this counted as a good tag.

The teacher sighed, pulling the glasses away from her face. "See me after class, Jacob."

One girl–one chubby girl with no makeup and a thick chin that covered her neck–was smiling, absolutely beaming at me. I smiled back at her. No one else seemed to care. I returned to my seat, ducking behind my backpack.

Too much adrenaline. Couldn't handle seeing my friends from Broadway, not yet. Someone might want me to tag them; too much to deal with, after my day.

I skipped out on the teacher's invitation to see her after class. Needed some fresh air, so I decided to walk home. Hot–always hot in this part of Texas. The last fresh, green colors of spring were baking away in the coming summer sun.

A few hundred yards from the school, walking in the same direction, was the plump girl who'd smiled at my performance earlier. Wondered if she'd talk to me.

"Hey," I said, breath coming in heavy huffs from jogging to catch up. "I'm Jacob. What's your name?"

"Hey," she answered, smiling at me. A pretty face—perfect teeth, glowing smile. Eyes and hair a deep brown. No makeup, no earrings, no need. Everything clean, simple. "I'm Nora."

"So, how do you like Mrs. Kerrigan's class?"

"It's okay," she said. "More interesting today than usual."

"Oh yeah?" I asked.

"I know what you were doing in there—I know that wasn't a real book. I gotta admit, that was pretty cool. Y'know, I kinda feel the same way half the time. Not the clothes, I mean, but people judging me for how I look."

"Why's that?"

"Don't play dumb," the plump girl accused. I shrugged; we walked five minutes without a word.

"So, where are you going?" I tried to resurrect the conversation, not sure what I'd done wrong.

"To the store," she said.

"I walk this way, too, sometimes."

"To the trailer park, right?" she asked.

"Yeah, the trailer park." The words came out stronger than I'd expected. Too used to being teased. She must have sensed it, because we were quiet for another five minutes.

I stared straight ahead while we walked another hundred yards. The red and white sign of Dairy Queen came into view.

"This is where I wait for my dad," she said.

"The ice cream is good here."

"What about it?" Hand on her hip.

"Nothing. I just...I just like it," I stammered. Don't mention food, ever—got it.

She stopped outside the fast food restaurant. I stopped too; I didn't want to leave her, not yet.

"When does your dad come to get you? He doesn't mind you waiting alone?"

"It's just for a little while; my mom is in the hospital."

"What's wrong with her?" I asked.

"She has cancer."

"Oh." I didn't know what else to say. In the struggle to come up with something nice, one of the most awkward sentences of my life surfaced: "Well, hey, having your mom die isn't too bad. My mom is dead, and I'm okay."

Nora looked at me, shocked, and began crying. I turned and walked away, fast.

7. Other people

Now

" —**J**ACOB THORKE," A GUARD CALLS. I awaken with a jolt, memories extinguished by fluorescent lights.

"Yeah?" I ask, stretching my neck.

"Come with me."

The guard opens the gate and I step through. There's a strange moment where he focuses on locking the cell again and I'm just looking around, thinking about escaping. He finishes and leads me deeper into the jail.

It's possible another member of the Six is imprisoned here. Not sure, but I might walk by him any moment. Kent Gimble.

The path the guard chooses—a winding one, worming through dark bowels of the jail—is meant to scare me, I believe. We end our tour in a room so small I can't imagine the space is designed for two, but the twin metal chairs force me to accept it.

I sit in the tiny chamber for what seems another eternity. Caught in limbo, between identities. In jail, men become new people, just to survive. I've got no trouble with that. Nothing keeps me from becoming whoever I need to be. David taught me well.

A few moments later, the door opens. The counselor assigned to me five years ago by the state—Mr. Aschen—fills the frame. The detective from before stands in the rear, badge reflecting the wan lights of the hall.

"Jacob Thorke, right now you're here as a witness. We've got forty-eight hours to decide if we want to let you go home as one, or if you'll be staying here with us as a suspect," the detective says. "We want to hear your version of events. Now, Mr. Aschen assures us he can get your full cooperation in telling us what led to the death of David Bloom. Because of your age, and because of your history, I'm allowing him to interview you—for now—until we make a final decision about your status here. I expect you to communicate honestly with us. A boy is dead, and we need to know what happened."

When I say nothing, the detective only nods and mumbles a few words to Mr. Aschen.

My counselor enters, a bulging folder in one hand, and closes the door. The familiar widow's peak points boldly down his forehead, directing attention to the long, narrow nose and tight mouth below.

Our knees are practically touching in the cramped space. The chamber feels a bit like a confessional.

"It's not so bad," Mr. Aschen says, forever an optimist, taking great pains to cross one leg over the other. A set of notes rests on his lap. He retrieves a pen—black and silver, elegant—and holds it between two fingers. "Bigger than my first office."

"They just want me to confess." I point my chin at the camera in the corner of the room. "There's no evidence. They think I'm more likely to confess to you."

"They also don't have any witnesses, Jacob, and you could be one. You're painting this picture."

"Is all that paper really about me, or is it just to make you look prepared?" I ask, staring at the thick manila folder in his lap.

Mr. Aschen responds with his infinitely patient grin. "I brought real notes. These are David's notes, and Emily's, and Cameron's, and Kent's, and Steven's. Yours are here, too. "

"Well, where do you want to start?"

"How did David die?" he asks. "And be honest, Jacob. Detectives in another room are watching all this, checking your facts, calling the people you mention. They're going to be listening very closely to what you say."

I shrug. "I'd almost rather be talking to them. You're going to try and convince me this is all David's fault, somehow. You always do. Look, I told the detective how David died. Someone in a mask pushed him off the water tower."

He folds his arms. "But, there's more to it," Mr. Aschen says gravely.

"There's more," I agree. "And you don't believe what I've told you, anyway."

"David is dead now, Jacob. It's time to focus on yourself and what you're going to do with the rest of your life. Are you going to put yourself in prison, or not?" I can smell the stale coffee on his breath. "Was this self-defense, Jacob? Did David attack you?"

"Never! Come on, David was always great to me."

"Great to you. What about everyone else?"

I lean back, wipe my palm across my face. "David didn't have a lot of respect for other people. People who weren't his friends, I mean. You know? But, they never had any respect for us, either. We were the novelty, we were the poor kids. At the end of it all, I think we can safely blame the death of David Bloom on other people."

8. No exit

Freshman year

HIGH SCHOOL WAS NOT AN IMPROVEMENT—being the youngest again stacked the odds against me, opened up the field. Sometimes, I had to avoid the bus stop; that meant riding my bike to school, then being late and sweaty. Teachers didn't help. Even though I mainly tried to avoid fights, I'd end up punished for being tardy, or for not paying attention. Hard to pay attention and watch my back at the same time.

The worst detentions came on Friday afternoon. Partly because of where they were held, but mostly because it was filled with the same people I'd gotten in trouble trying to avoid. We were supposed to meet in one of the extracurricular facilities a few hundred feet away from the main campus—small, cheap, standalone buildings.

The detention hall served a number of purposes, one of which was as a dark room for the photography class. Just walking up, knowing what I was in for—it was a struggle of willpower. The lack of windows made it a shit place to spend two hours. I'd wasted a lot of time in that little cage.

David had not. He never got caught for his crimes, and so I was surprised to find him leaning against the side of the shed.

"What's up?" I asked.

He turned, uncrossed his arms and stood straight. "Experimenting."

The door swung open; a bulky coach stood within, hand on the doorknob. Before I could say another word to David—who stood out of view—I was ushered inside.

The detention monitor extended his hand, motioning for my cell phone.

"I don't have one," I said. He relented.

Maybe ten students in attendance, freshmen through seniors. I knew a few personally: some of my worst enemies.

"White trash," someone barked out in fake coughs as I sat in the corner. The coach looked up, searching for the offender, and the coughing stopped.

I settled in for a long afternoon.

Fifteen minutes in, a cell phone chirped. Everyone looked around, eager to find the culprit—but the monitor was the guilty party. He glanced at his phone, looking shocked, then worried, fidgeting for a few moments.

His eyes jumped between the door, us, and his phone. Little surge of excitement: something was happening. Would we get out early?

"Excuse me," the coach said. "I've had a personal emergency. Someone will be here to replace me in a couple of minutes, just sit tight. They will be here any second."

The coach shoved the door open and exited.

Could hardly believe the luck. My fellow inmates turned in their chairs, making eye contact and smiling in disbelief. A few began picking up their backpacks, ready to leave.

Then the lights went out.

The door opened and closed; abyssal blackness. I couldn't see the desk in front of me.

That moment of tension. Quick blackout, or long? Nothing to do but sit perfectly still.

"Hey!" a baritone voice shouted. "Hey, turn the light back on."

No response. Might as well be blind. The sounds were just abstract notions coming through this all-encompassing dark.

"I'll get it." I heard a voice near the door get up, followed by the sound of stumbling. A desk squeaked across the floor; a chair toppled. The impotent clicks of a dead switch.

Heard a knob twisted; a door shaken against its frame.

"The door is locked." Panic rising. Then, again, twice as loud: "It's locked!"

"Hey! Who locked us in here?" The baritone voice took on a threatening tone.

"Cell phones," a voice came from the black. "We can call out."

I heard a series of shuffling sounds as the objects on the teacher's desk were knocked all over the floor. I could make out pens falling, and papers, but nothing that might be a box of cell phones.

"They're gone." The voice confirmed what we all instinctively knew by now: We were trapped together.

The first few minutes were chaos. The big bass-filled voice in the room raged uncontrollably: "Let me out," he commanded. "I'm gonna kill whoever did this, I don't even care. Let me out!"

He must've rose from his chair. Feet slid across the cement floor. The sound of a foot hitting a desk, followed by the firm *thwak* of something solid—a knee, a skull—smacking against something even more solid—a table, a floor. A five second pause, then "Christ, my head" in a low groan.

I sat in my desk in the corner, hands gripping the wood. Trapped. I suspected David had something to do with this, so I only wanted to watch.

As we settled into the void, it became impossible to ignore that someone was crying. A boy's voice. It didn't let up, growing louder by the minute, vocalizing our shared despair. We grew quiet, listening, feeling the awkwardness rise. By the time the sobbing voice spoke, it was the only sound in the room. "Guys, this is embarrassing, but I'm nyctophobic." The boy's words came out cracked and chipped.

The baritone voice: "What the hell does that mean?"

"He's afraid of the dark," a female voice sang forth.

"What kind of pussy is afraid of the dark?" The baritone.

"It's a real medical condition." The tremulous voice of the nyctophobe. "I think I'm gonna pass out."

"Take deep breaths," the concerned female voice came again. "Put your head between your knees."

"Please, talk to me." The scared voice got softer.

"Okay," the girl said. "What do you want to know?"

"I don't care, anything. Talk to me. I don't think I know you. Which one are you? What do you look like?"

"Umm, y'know..." the female reply came. "Blonde hair, I'm skinny, I have green eyes. Pretty, I guess. I mean, not like, beautiful or anything. I'd say I'm pretty, though."

Someone scoffed sarcastically.

"Oh my God, who made that sound when I said I was pretty?" the female voice asked. "Do you even know who's talking right now?"

Another chuckle.

"Well, I *am* pretty," she reassured us. "If I'm not pretty, why do I have so many boyfriends?"

"Technically, that just means you're easy," said a dry voice from the back. Enter a new character—the smartass.

"Shut up, she *is* pretty." A second female voice, this one supporting the first. The personalities of the darkness were splitting and dividing schizophrenically.

"I think you're hot," the baritone voice spoke again.

"You're just trying to get laid," the smartass said.

"Well then, what do *you* look like?" The first girl, the one whose beauty was challenged.

Silence.

"See? Not so easy, is it?" The second female voice.

"Well, you're not pretty in the dark," a new voice said. "Technically, you don't look like anything."

Someone interrupted: "Would you stop arguing?" The crying voice again, the boy with the phobia. "You're making it worse."

Silence.

Felt like we'd been trapped for hours.

"I think I'm going to have a heart attack." The nyctophobe again.

"If he gets seriously hurt, what are we going to do?" One of the girls.

"Sit here and listen to him die," the smartass answered. "What can we do?"

"Don't say that. That's not helping." Female.

"Okay, everyone, let's stand up. Link arms. We'll move as a unit and find our way out of here." Baritone.

"Stupid," murmured the darkness.

"Who said that?" The baritone voice got loud again, more commanding. "You tell me, I'll smack the shit out of you, I don't care how dark it is."

"I think we should do what he says," said one of the girls.

"Cheerleaders and jocks, always sticking together. What's the point? We're locked in here. Linking arms isn't going to fix anything. We might be in here all weekend. Better just chill out and try to relax." Smartass.

The nyctophobe let out a pitiful whimper. "This is like my worst nightmare coming true."

"You're a coward," a boy accused. The anonymous sound of the darkness again; an indistinct male voice I hadn't placed yet.

A second voice began sobbing, creating a pathetic chorus.

"Screw this. I'm gonna get us out of here," baritone said.

"You're not strong or smart enough to get us out of here," the darkness informed; another voice without an identity. Just data, hanging there.

Silence.

An indeterminable length of time later, a voice mewed forth.

"I am pretty, right?" she asked. The voice of the girl who'd been mocked for her claims earlier.

"Yes, you are beautiful." The second female voice.

"Maybe a six," the darkness said. "Seven, if I was drunk."

"Who said that?" the female demanded, sounding frantic.

Silence.

"What will we do for water?" the darkness asked. "If we're in here for the weekend, we might dehydrate. We could die. Especially if you keep crying."

A second person's weeping joined the first, then a third. The chamber became a symphony of fear-wracked whimpering. Sounded like a jungle at midnight: Panicked panting, pocked by short howls of sorrow. Too loud in here; the sound was crushing. One voice in particular sounded terrified, sobbing relentlessly.

"I bet I could kick down the door," the baritone voice said.

"Are you kidding me?" the smart-ass responded. "It's metal. Besides, you're not that big."

"Big enough to kick your ass."

"You wouldn't be saying that if the lights were on. You're weak." That unidentified voice, prodding us again.

Motion; someone stood and tried to move across the room. Tables shifted, squealing along the linoleum floor. Bodies collided, shouting erupted. "It's not me!" and "Get off me, asshole!" could be heard from minor players in the masquerade as each scrambled to get away from the rampaging baritone.

Then it stopped.

"See what I mean?" the darkness asked once the commotion ceased. "Weak."

"I'm not weak," the baritone insisted. "Ask any of my friends, they know me. I'm tough, seriously. I'm in detention for beating the shit out of that loser Patrick. Probably your friend."

"You think that makes you tough?" The first girl's voice. "That just makes you a jerk."

The baritone sighed, and that was louder than anything he could say—helplessness.

"Talk to me." The nyctophobe said. "I feel better when I can hear you talk."

"What do you want to know?" The second female, the supporter.

"I don't care, just talk. Tell me about yourself."

Silence. No one dared speak, after what'd happened to the others. The darkness was cruel.

Finally, someone stepped up: "I'll talk about myself." The smartass. "I'll tell you why I'm in detention. They caught me smoking behind the school. They thought I had a cigarette, but old-ass Ms. Melker didn't know it was weed. So, the way I figure, I actually got lucky with detention. This isn't so bad, considering."

"Oh wow, big bad boy, watch out," the first girl's voice sneered sarcastically.

The second female voice pitched in: "Doing drugs doesn't make you any cooler than beating up geeks."

"Do you ever think for yourself, or do you just echo whatever she says?" The smartass ignored the pretty girl and challenged the second one.

A response was mounted, but sputtered and died on the lips of the second girl.

I put my head down on the desk. The anger and fear in the room was suffocating. Felt like I'd been here for hours; couldn't stand the way everyone picked themselves apart in the dark. Why did this work in the light?

Silence.

"Please, talk to me," the quaking mess of the nyctophobe. "You can't understand how horrible this is for me. I can feel everything closing in, it's like the shadows are squeezing me. I can't breathe. Please, someone, let me know I'm not alone."

Moments passed. I held my breath, curiosity rising. No one spoke.

Silence.

Another ten, fifteen minutes gone. Seemed like everyone had given up trying to communicate: it only led to arguing, pain, and judgment. We just listened to the sniffling of the nyctophobe, waiting for him to die of a heart attack, or whatever happened when a panic attack got worse and worse.

Then, the sound we all dared to hope for—keys jingling in the door. We fell silent; no one dared move. Another jingle, and our suspicions were confirmed. Everyone burst into cries for help at once.

The door swung open. "What the hell is going on here?" the janitor asked.

A dozen explanations were thrown at him at once. My eyes stung from the invading sunlight as bodies began pushing their way through. Electric lights dazzled; I walked through the frame and into the world. Sun was setting; must have been inside for a couple of hours.

I turned and watched the people I'd been trapped with as they emerged, dazed, from the detention hall. Some voices were easy to place: the tallest, biggest boy was the baritone. The prettiest girl and her slightly-less-pretty friend followed—girls one and two. The smartass with his unkempt hair, patchy beard and glasses came next, along with a host of supporting characters who apparently never had the nerve to announce their presence.

While many noses and eyes were chafed and red, I couldn't pinpoint a person who might've been the nyctophobe. No one appeared so distraught they might be having a panic attack; they only looked defeated and depressed.

The last person stepped through. David, hands in his pockets, smile on his face.

"You..."

He smiled. "They weren't the same in there, were they? With the lights off, I mean. Like everyone started coming unglued."

"You put yourself in there. You planned this!" I accused. "Who were you?"

We walked side by side as night fell around us. At least it would be cool on our long walk to Broadway.

Something occurred to me. "You know, in church they say the devil makes us sin. I think he's a scapegoat. Hell could be all around us, you know? Sidewalks and street signs, but no mirrors. No mirrors in hell. People in hell can see everyone but themselves. Those people in that room didn't know who they were. They gotta ask someone else, and they never hear what they want to hear."

He was quiet for a long time, just watching me. Then he smiled. "I think you're right," David said. "You did all right, though."

"Is that was this was? Testing me? You're crazy," I said.

David began sniffling dramatically, breaking into fake sobs. The sound was familiar, and rightly so: I'd been listening to the constant crying for the last few hours.

The sobs stopped. "A little crazy," he said, smiling now.

"You were him," I accused.

He just smiled wider.

9. Father figures

Freshman year

I HAD ANOTHER RUN-IN WITH DAVID a few days later, right after school. I'd just gotten home, and I stalled outside with my fingers on the aluminum doorknob of my trailer. Two voices spoke within. One was Dad's, and the other familiar, but—the hot metal singed my skin, so I pulled away, cursing. Couldn't touch anything in Texas, once it got sunny. I wrapped my shirt around my hand and jerked the door open.

The second voice? David's. He sat across from my dad, leg folded, hands in his lap. Tall, lean and tan. He had a kind of handsomeness that was hard to hate, because it seemed unintentional.

"What's going on?" I asked the pair, little bit of disbelief choking me. Hadn't expected to see these two together. Felt weird; felt wrong.

"We were just chatting, is all," Dad said, somewhat defensively.

"Okay..." I murmured, setting my backpack down. *Whatever.*

"How was your day, Jacob?" David asked.

"Boring. Do you want to go hang out somewhere?"

"Oh, do you want to?" he asked, apparently surprised—as though it was totally normal to be in my home, talking to my dad.

"Well, I didn't mean to interrupt anything." I shoved the front door open and stepped out. David stood, shrugged at my father as if to say 'what's his problem?' and followed me outside.

He caught up to me as I walked across the park.

"Everything okay?"

"You have a good time in there?" I asked.

"Yeah, he's a nice guy. You should talk to him more often."

"I talk to him plenty," I said. "He's my *dad*."

The stones made a chewing noise as we walked across them, like teeth grinding down bone. "I'm not sure how you came from him," David said with hands behind his back, serene smile stamped on his face.

"What do you mean?"

"You've got this awareness, you know? You're different."

"I don't know."

David sped up, almost to where I couldn't notice it, except now I was following him across Broadway, and not the other way around.

"You notice things, is all. Things that other people don't notice. Like Eureka."

"You noticed Eureka," I replied. "You made the whole thing up."

"I was just trying to manipulate you," he admitted, shoulders slumped. "You're the one who kept playing. You're the one who likes it."

"It scares me," I said.

We crossed the park and reached David's trailer. Black bags of garbage surrounded it. Ms. Bloom sat on a plastic chair, smoking a cigarette. David's mom looked mechanical in an electronic world. Like something from the past century, run by ropes and pulleys, rusted and decrepit. Her arm shook with the effort of cranking the smoldering bit of cancer up to her thin, dry lips.

"I want to show you something," David said to me.

We approached his mother. Ms. Bloom stared up at us with wide, startled eyes; the same deep brown as David's, but milk-soaked. "Hey, Mom," he said.

Ms. Bloom narrowed those enormous eyes suspiciously, then swiveled her head left and right, seemingly relieved to find she was home. Her mouth opened; the dark tar of cigarettes greased her teeth. "Did the landlord send you?" she asked.

I held my breath and searched David's face for answers.

"He wanted to tell you that you're beautiful. So beautiful that you never have to pay rent again," David answered.

Ms. Bloom smiled, chipped gears in her brain finding leverage and twisting the contraption around for another revolution. David's message was stored in a broken bin from which it would soon come tumbling out, only to be replaced again—a perpetual motion which wore down the cogs of the machine to useless nubs.

We stood for a few moments, and then her smile passed. She stared blankly ahead at her son, unrecognizing, waiting for him to say something else. David turned, tugging my arm to draw me away.

"Alzheimer's," he explained as we walked into the forest behind the trailer. "Sometimes she remembers me. Usually not."

"That's horrible. I'm sorry."

"Not your fault. Not anyone's fault, just life."

I looked back at her. She'd reset, and looked just like we found her. Oblivious. "It's like dying every minute. Forgetting it all, like it never happened in the first place, over and over."

"There you go, noticing things again," David said.

10. Grounded

Now

"DAVID WAS A SOCIOPATH, JACOB. He probably didn't realize it was strange to be in your dad's house. He had no sense of personal boundaries. He didn't even know what other people were, really," Mr. Aschen says.

"He just didn't know what a parent was—why would he?"

Mr. Aschen holds the pen in both hands, twisting it against the cap. It's the way he gets when he wants to say something, but knows he shouldn't.

"Just say it," I prompt, lifting my palms to the cell around us. "I think we're past pretending you're going to do a good job, here."

"I'm upset that David is dead. I feel partly responsible, of course: I'm the only counselor he saw, and I certainly didn't improve his situation," he says. "But I've always felt like you had the best chance, out of everyone to come from that mess. You're the one that reached out for help. That's why I figured you'd want to tell us how David died, you know?"

I look up at the camera mounted in the corner of the room while I speak. "You won't understand David's death if you don't understand our situation. Being poor wasn't enough; we also had the landlord to deal with. He changed everything. When you say I helped my friends, you're talking about junior year, right?"

"When you called the police, yes." He pushes his glasses up onto the bridge of his nose. "You saved them all, really."

"I have a story about that, too."

⸺ ∾ ⸺

Junior year

Spiked hair; swords big as surfboards. Save screens and main themes—electric guitars only played on the boss fights; that's how I knew when things were serious. Pixels and pigments, pixies and pygmies.

Or space marines with guns like leaf blowers, jet packs on backs, hold the grenades for no more than two seconds, save shotgun ammo for the little fast ones. Circle strafing contests of skill. Ballistic trajectory determined on balance sheets, digital sports played out by mathletes.

Really, it was about getting our minds the hell out of Broadway. I played the video games in Steven's trailer a few times a week. Everything was used, bought from a pawn shop, but we didn't mind.

My glasses-clad friend excelled in the virtual realm. "I beat David three out of five yesterday," Steven said.

I looked away from the screen long enough to cast an unimpressed glance at him. "Yeah, so? David could beat you in real life."

Steven grunted, then settled the argument with another headshot. My ninth loss in a row.

"Play again?" he asked.

"So you can keep beating me?" I dropped the controller.

"It's fun." Steven started another game anyway. My half of the screen stared out, unmoving, while his half went on the hunt.

"Fun for you," I stood and looked out the yellowed window. The landlord's trailer sat a dozen feet away, biggest one on the biggest plot, dominating the park. Constant reminder. "You see him lately?"

Steven turned. "This morning, I could hear him snoring out my window. Passed out on his lawn chair again. Someday I'm gonna turn the sprinkler on him."

"Whatever you say."

He smiled. The screen's image reflected in the bulbous lenses of his glasses; my character filled his frames. Steven pulled the trigger. My avatar's head exploded in a mess of red polygons.

"Would you really mess with Kent's dad?" I asked, forehead pressed against the window.

Steven began to hunt for my new spawning place. "Fucking menace, not to mention his mongoloid son. You can't tell me the world wouldn't be a better place without Mr. Gimble. You know he used to 'play' with Cameron, right?" Our two halves of the screen met. Three shots to the chest, and my half went red again.

Suspected it. Years ago—the dirty package of sugar in Cameron's hand, the landlord waiting for her. It made sense, even though it made me feel sick. 'Menace' was right.

"Why does he get away with it?" I asked.

Steven turned and shrugged. "Because he's huge. Because he has guns? Because this is the cheapest place to live in Kingwood, and he could kick our parents out if he wanted?"

"Or is it because we don't do anything about it?" I asked, running my finger through the dust collected on the window blind. "I mean, how can we really say he's gotten away with anything, if no one has ever tried to stop him?"

Steven turned back to his game, hunting my avatar down again.

"What do you think he *really* deserves?" I challenged. He put down the controller, stared up at me. "I mean, if you had to do something."

Didn't even have to say it; he just knew. I'd been 'it' since last week.

The trailer rocked with our sudden movement. I jumped across the living room, hand extended, brushing Steven's leg as he scrambled up and over the couch, laughing.

"Tag," I hollered.

Steven lay on the floor. He straightened the thick black frames on his face and ran a hand through his hair.

"Go ahead," I said. "Do it. Stop talking about how this place should be. Let's change it."

He glanced around the apartment, big eyes focusing on one thing then another, searching for some way to change his life in the next fifteen minutes.

Legs carried him across the trailer, arm reached for the phone on the wall. Fingers dialed three digits, then stopped.

There was only one possibility: nine-one-one.

"Hello, officer? Yeah; I live in Broadway Trailer Park. The landlord here, Mr. Gimble—he's molests this girl, Cameron. Her mom lets it happen." Steven's voice quaked. He stared at the phone, like the receiver had just come alive in his hand. He slammed it back down on its stand.

I stood, jaw hanging open. "I'm outta here. Tell the police I said 'hi.'"

Three days passed before an unusual number of well-dressed adults began snooping around Broadway. Things were inconspicuous at first: a man with a clipboard talking to a few parents. Then the next week, a man and a woman. Then a man, a woman, a police officer, and a German Shepherd.

One morning: pandemonium. The sound of car doors slamming and unfamiliar adult voices speaking in commanding tones. The warble of walkie-talkies. I peeked through the worn bed sheet covering my window and saw a number of official-looking men and women getting out of police cruisers and black Suburbans.

I hurried to the living room, where my father slept. "Dad? Hey, wake up," I said, nudging him. "Some guys are coming over."

"No friends over," he mumbled. "Sleeping."

"No, Dad. They're grownups. They're all over the park. I think they're cops or something."

This woke him up in a hurry. Dad leaned forward with a tremendous groan. He'd been lying on the bed/couch/dinner table at the far end of the trailer next to our best TV—his nest. He lumbered shakily from the bed, steadying his legs by pressing against the thin walls.

Dad brushed his teeth, smoothed his long mustache, then closed our tiny bathroom door. The shower ran for a few seconds and, in less than a minute, he returned.

There was a knock on the trailer door.

I opened our home to a tall black man with a clipboard. As soon as the door swung open, he pushed a shoulder in and looked around the living space.

"Hi. What can I do for you?" Dad asked. Super polite, now.

"Hello, my name is Zach. I'm with CPS," Zach said in the same fake-friendly voice doctors used.

I cocked an eyebrow at him.

"Child Protective Services," he explained.

"Jacob, don't bug the man," Dad said with a nod. "What can I do for you? Nothing is wrong, I hope." Every consonant hit. Perfect elocution.

Zach cleared his throat as if to say, 'nothing is under par, but yes, everything is wrong.' Still, he continued in the same professional tone: "It's not about you. We just want to talk about your neighbors. Is there a place we can speak in private?"

"Sure. Jacob, why don't you go out and do something?" Then Dad cast a glance at Zach. "Something safe. Go somewhere supervised."

There was more of the same outside. It was like a goddamn raid —a very polite one, but a raid. Cops at every trailer.

I crossed the park in a daze. Couldn't believe what I was seeing. Mr. Gimble was being led into a police car. Fat arms barely reached behind his back; it took two sets of handcuffs linked together to bind them. The landlord faced the ground with the same sad look as when I caught him sleeping outside the trailer. Not rage or denial or disbelief, but sadness.

Kent wiped tears from his eyes. He stood in front of the mobile home where two of the CPS women held him back as he tried to get to his dad.

Cameron and Steven stood in an embrace, each crying onto the other's shoulder. More police cars pulled up; before I could ask why

Steven was crying, I watched an officer lead his dad toward one of the arriving cruisers.

His walk of shame was interrupted by a howl from across the trailer park. Two policemen dragged Cameron's mom, shirt ripped, drooling, kicking, and cursing to the nearest cruisers. She bit into her handler's knuckles and was dropped face-first into the ground with a dull thud. Ms. Merrill screamed as officers locked her cuffs into place, then bound her feet as well.

The cops carried Cameron's mom like a carcass, one with an arm looped around her arms and another holding her legs, nose dangling inches from the ground. She screeched incomprehensibly, howling harpy. Cameron stared, eyes wide and mouth agape.

A final figure was led down Broadway's catwalk of shame: an older woman with a confused expression on her face. Automaton, brittle like rusted iron. Ms. Bloom put up no struggle as she was led into a police cruiser.

I blame the death of David Bloom on the fact that no matter what, everything changes.

[sic]

11. Other people's dads

Junior year

WATER FROM THE LAKE in Nora's backyard sat in little beads on my arm. I blew on the droplets; they trembled in the sun, light dancing across my skin.

"So, wait, how did everyone's parents end up in jail?"

Good question, Nora.

"Cameron was her mom's rent payment; she was in on the whole thing. We told them that when we called the cops. When they got there, they went into every trailer, asked questions, dug around. Didn't take them long to realize David's mom was so sick he's the one taking care of her, not the other way around. Steven's dad was just bad luck—there was a roach in the ashtray, some weed. Apparently that's enough for CPS."

"What are all your friends going to do if their parents are in jail?"

"They're at—I don't know. I went there; it was like a camp. They sleep in bunks, with like ten other people in the room. Sucks."

"When do they go home?"

"Never? They're fifteen, sixteen. No one is going to adopt someone that old. It's weird. I thought everything was normal in Broadway—crappy, but normal. Then the cops come in, and they're totally shocked by what we were going through. Even my dad had to go to court. Makes you feel like—I don't know. It's messed up to have someone see your life and be like 'Oh my God, you poor thing, how did you survive?' Plus, it's kinda too late, you know? We already survived it. I'm glad Mr. Gimble is going to prison, but the damage is done."

51

"I'm sorry, Jacob," Nora said.

Grackles circled overhead, laughing noisily. I'd been visiting her house a lot, lately. Where else was there to go?

I continued: "We all have to go to counseling. My dad was so pissed about it. They think that Mr. Gimble might have screwed with us all, so we should see this psychologist in case we're crazy. And I get in there, and the therapist already knows about this game we play. It's all he wants to talk about."

"What game?" she asked, cheeks and nose red from the sun.

"I've never told anyone from school about this before."

"Well, what is it?" She stretched the black t-shirt—the one that wasn't see-through when it got wet, the one she always wore when she was swimming—over her knees.

"You don't want to know," I said. "You won't get it."

Nora rolled her head back, smiling at the sky. "I *do* want to know. Come on, you can't say something like that and not explain it, dork."

"Okay, fine. So, someone tags you. Like, David in this case—and you have to change your life in the next fifteen minutes. You have to do anything other than what you planned on doing. If you were going to go to school, don't go to school. If you were going to let the landlord ruin your life, don't let him."

Nora said nothing. I continued: "Then you're 'it' and you can tag one of the other players, and they have to do the same. Anyway, the counselor is not crazy about it."

She bit her bottom lip, then spoke: "You should listen to your counselor; the game sounds...kinda stupid."

"I don't think it's stupid. Sometimes the things we're afraid of doing need to be done most."

"Okay, so maybe *once*." She drank from a jam jar full of iced tea. "Or even twice. But how do you make plans? How do you get stuff done?"

"That's not the point, though."

"Not the point you want to make, you mean," Nora said. "Why screw up your future?" She opened her hands at the lake below us, at the wooden deck where we sat.

"Because my future sucks. Have you seen my life? Most high school students don't go see a state-appointed counselor. Not everyone lives on the lake and has a nice dad who makes them lunch."

Nora's father smiled from behind expansive windows, where he washed the dishes from the sandwiches he'd made us.

"You have to work hard to get the things you want," Nora said.

"Yeah? Did you work really hard to be born in this house, with a nice dad who has money?"

"My dad did! It sounds like you just don't want to try," she snapped. Then Nora shook her head, seeming to reconsider. "Sorry."

"I'm sorry I even told you about it." My throat tightened around the words. "Can't one person on this planet agree with me?"

"I would never agree with you for the sake of agreeing, Jacob. I actually *care* about you," Nora said.

This must be true, but neither of us ever voiced it until that moment. I couldn't stay mad. "C'mon, let's go inside."

12. Sport

Junior year

LUNCHTIME, HIGH SCHOOL. Another daily battleground. Forced to stand stupid at the watering hole, waiting to get my tray filled—carrots, mashed potatoes, fish sticks. In the untamed wilderness of the cafeteria, the snobs stalked their prey slowly.

Girls with sequins like snake scales. Brightly-painted vixens with toxins. Only a few words, except they sunk into you like venom, eating you from the inside out while she batted innocent eyes.

The boys were different. Pack predators. The bravest traded turns, getting closer each time, building off each other's excitement until one drew blood. They always stopped, at least for a moment, when that blood showed. It was a choice: respond like a person, or an animal.

Always, animal.

An attack was coming. I had enough experience to read the signs. I could already hear the little hyena giggles, building as courage grew and the game intensified. The lunch line moved slowly, so I was trapped. Laughter increased as food was slopped onto my plate. Build that bloodlust to a boil, then:

"Hey, Jake," the tallest of the five said, after some prodding from his friends.

"What?" Trying not to show emotion. Yet.

"I'm having a party. I was going to invite you—what's your number? I'll text you." More snickering. Didn't have a cell phone. Probably one of ten kids in the school who could say that.

Still, this was the bait. It'd be stupid to react; that was part of their game. Make it look like my fault. I ignored them.

The boy who initiated contact withdrew a cell phone. The flat, vibrant panel bathed his hand in healing light.

I wanted one, but those kinds of things weren't meant for me.

"Whatever," I mumbled, and turned around to face the lunch lady.

I wasn't taking the bait. Now they had a choice: back off, or go for blood.

They crowded around me in a semicircle, drawing closer.

"Look at his shoes," a boy from the group said loudly, pointing. My two-year-old Goodwill sneakers were coated in trailer-park muck. "Did you have to climb a telephone pole to pull those down?"

Laughter. Students in the line in front of me turned to watch this unfold; the event began to cross the threshold.

"*Who* are Def Leopard?" asked one of the vipers in the back. To be honest, I wasn't sure either. It was my dad's shirt.

"Gross," another girl murmured.

Steven, Kent and Cameron got up from our table and walked over. The three stood behind me; I'd done the same for them before.

"Why do you guys do this?" Kent asked, stepping in front of me and looking down at the greasy, spiked hair of the one who called out my shoes.

"Why do you screw your cousin?" a kid from the rear of the group quipped, protected by the layer of bodies between him and Kent.

Someone tugged at my sleeve and I turned, frustrated by the distraction. Cameron pulled on my shirt.

"What?" I hissed.

"Tag. You're 'it,'" she murmured.

Christ. Of course. Fifteen minutes to change.

I didn't even think about it—any change would do; I was sick of everything. I turned and knocked the cell phone out of the closest boy's hand, sending the device clattering across the ground. Now the entire cafeteria sat riveted.

"You think all this bullshit makes you better than me?" I asked him, stepping up as he stared in disbelief at the phone, which scraped across the linoleum floor. "You think having all this stuff matters? It's just junk your mom bought you."

"At least I've got a mom." The punk murmured murder.

My hand flew forward, balling into a fist the moment before my knuckles hit his lip. I twisted the fabric of his shirt around one hand, preparing to punch again. He flinched, head twisted away.

"I don't care. I don't care about any of this shit—you, your clothes, or your phone. Play with your fucking toys, I'll be over here *evolving*." I shoved him again. The bully stumbled into the pack; I stepped through them, made it ten feet and was grabbed by a teacher.

I watched our audience as she dragged me to the office. For the first time, something other than pity and disgust shone in the eyes of other students. *Respect.*

Eureka.

13. The quack

Junior year

"STUPID BARBIE BITCHES," Nora spat as she stalked off. I struggled to keep up with her. "Bobble-headed trolls...makeup by DuPont. Snotty, snobby, slutty, *skinny...*" she stuttered and stopped. She'd been waiting for the bus with me when two slimmer, more popular girls targeted her.

"Hey, it's all right. Don't worry about them. What they think of you doesn't matter—you're great," I said.

"I want to punch each of them in the throat. Line them up, Jacob, so I can start punching throats."

"I'll go grab one," I joked, turning back to the school. "I'll hold her arms, you handle the throat-punching."

Eyes rolled. She groaned and stopped walking, shoulders slumped. "How do you deal with it?"

We locked eyes. "You know how I handle this," I said.

"Don't start on that Eureka crap again." She stretched her hands out across tight shorts, pulling them further down her thighs. We watched the bus stop from fifty feet away.

"Maybe Eureka would do you some good."

"What are you saying, Jacob? I need to change?"

Couldn't go there. I could see she was uncomfortable with her own body—but how was I supposed to tell her that? If I even suggested it, she'd go all defensive.

I tried something different: "I like you how you are. I always have, you're awesome. If you were just like every one of those other girls in there," I motioned toward the high school, "I wouldn't even want to talk to you. And what would you do without me?"

"I'd have one less person to worry about. Jesus, did you even start Ms. Lachey's report? You know it's like forty percent of your grade, right?"

"Let's not focus on the ungodly number of things wrong with me. I'm too easy of a target. You're damn near perfect, Nora—you're smart, you're funny. I'm just saying, you can do anything you want. You can just change it, right now."

"I know," she said. "And that's sweet, really. Sometimes, I wonder what I'm missing. The friends, the parties, all that stuff. Being popular...but could you imagine *my* fat ass with a boyfriend?" she asked, snorting at herself. "I'd probably crush him."

"I'd go out with you," I said. The words tumbled out awkwardly; she cocked an eyebrow. We stood and stared at each other for five, ten seconds—felt like ten minutes—until she smiled.

The growling of a diesel engine saved me from a follow-up. "I've got stupid Mr. Aschen today, so I'll call you later tonight, all right?" I yelled as I got in line for the bus.

Nora nodded, still smiling. "You got this," she reassured me.

My legs swung back and forth under the chair. I stared idly at paintings of beaches, lakes, birds, and other calming crap. What sort of artist was so goddamn boring, they'd spend hours working on pictures of ducks chilling in a pond? What was that supposed to *do?*

What does this piece mean to you? The critic would ask the artist, hand on chin, ready to be impressed.

I like ducks, the artist would answer. *They go 'quack.'*

Another half-hour spent in the waiting room of Mr. Aschen's office. Another half-hour wasted.

David and Steven sat on either side of me. Kent was inside, apparently going into overtime. He was forty minutes into a thirty minute session, which meant we'd all be staying later than we wanted.

"Probably admitting he can't read," Steven mumbled. David snickered.

"Shouldn't be saying anything," David muttered. "Tell the shrink what he wants to hear, get in and out. Waste of my time."

I rubbed my forehead. Being trapped in between all this soothing bullshit gave me a headache. I hated that outside of school, this was the only time I saw the Six.

The door opened and we fell silent. Kent trudged out, eyes misty. Steven snickered; Kent jumped at the smaller boy in mock attack. It worked and he flinched, practically folding between the slats of his chair. Kent smirked and kept walking out the door.

Mr. Aschen called from his office: "David? Are you ready to talk with me?"

"Why do you even ask? Trying to trick me into thinking I have a choice?" David asked as he trudged over to the counselor. They entered the office; the door closed.

Steven leaned forward. "Hey, man. I need your help."

"What?" I folded my arms across my chest.

"Kent is making my life hell." He pulled up his shirt; three purple bruises marked his abs. "I can't handle this, man. Do you know what it's like having to live with him? School is bad enough; now home is worse."

"You did call the cops on his dad," I reminded him.

He fell back into his chair, wet sheen over his eyes. "Don't blame all this on me! You know you wanted this to happen. You tagged me, didn't you? Plus, in my head—I thought Kent would be gone and I would still be home. It's easy on you; you never have to see him."

"What am I supposed to do? Pretend I called the cops?"

"Exactly," Steven said. "Take the blame."

"I can't, man," I said. "I mean, I feel bad—and I'm glad Mr. Gimble is gone, but you know..."

"Do you know what I'm going through? Fuck." He clutched his head. "I tried to do everyone a favor. Get rid of the landlord—everyone wanted it. We all know he was a piece of shit. I did the right thing. Then they find a roach in my dad's ashtray. Then we've got a drug dog tearing up the trailer, and they find his stash. So, who cares if they stepped on my Playstation, right? Because they're taking me with them. Apparently, I can't live by myself. I'm sixteen! Bullshit. And, my dad was fine. But David and Cameron, you know —his mom completely lost it. Her mom loaned her out for rent— someone needed to shine the light on all that shit. I'm glad this happened, but goddamn if it doesn't hurt. Everyone dragged out of their homes...I didn't plan on that. You gotta help me carry this."

How was I supposed to answer? Everything he said was true.

Steven stood. "How about you take the blame for the same reason I went through with it?"

A cold chill crept up the base of my spine. I didn't try to run. "Come on, don't do this." Weak objection.

Steven stepped across the room and touched me on the arm, where my hand clenched the chair. "Tag."

"Are you serious?"

"Hey, man—you get to enjoy life without the landlord, right? Well, pay your part for it. Please."

Shit. I did feel bad for him. I could imagine Steven, miserable at home and at school, constantly being picked on by someone. And in a way, he had a point. Nothing in Broadway was right. Eureka changed it all.

No real choice, then. Not even a real tag; just a manipulation. But, he needed my help.

I stood and marched out of the office. Kent waited outside, hugging legs to chest, chubby jowls spread out across the knees where his head rested.

I sat down. "Hey, man," I said.

"Hey," he responded, face sullen, eyes down.

"Sorry about all this." Poor Kent. He might be a little violent, but with a dad like his—whose fault was that?

Kent nodded, yellow bangs of his bowl-cut grown out long enough to reach his eyebrows. "You shouldn't feel sorry; it's not your fault." He saw an ant on the cement below him, and smashed it with his thumb. "I hate foster care. It's like school. My whole life is school."

I twisted around and glanced at Steven, who stared through the window inside, pointing at his watch.

"I need to tell you something," I said. "Please don't beat the crap out of me after I do."

Kent sniffed, then turned to look at me. "What?"

I told my lie: "This is my fault. You've been blaming Steven, but I'm the one who called the police. We were in Steven's trailer and he tagged me. I'm sorry. I didn't know this would happen. I just wanted to protect Cameron."

He watched me, searching my face for something. In truth, I did feel partly responsible, and so it wasn't hard to commit to the lie.

"So...we okay?" I prodded, after he just kept staring.

The landlord's son stood, pushed the bangs out of his eyes. Staring up at him really drove home how tall he was, how big. At least a hundred pounds on me. Kent looked at the parking lot, laughed. No humor in it.

I didn't have a chance to hear what came next. The door to the counselor's office swung open. David stormed out, practically leaping over Kent and I. Mr. Aschen came through the door and—

14. Blackbird

Now

M R. ASCHEN FINISHES THE SENTENCE for his past self: "—I shouted 'David, there's more to discuss.' But I was wrong. David's problem was obvious from the first time he opened his mouth—" He's interrupted by the sound of a woman screaming savagely. We turn to stare out the small square window of the interview room.

The howling is severe, coming from a small wretch who bites and scratches at the three guards trying to control her. Spiny hands cling to any surface they can find purchase; limbs extend insect-like, roach clinging to drain.

A guard grabs her arm but she wrenches free, running down the hallway, away from her captors. When she reaches the door at the other end and it won't open, she claws at the barrier. No luck; the men corner her and wrestle her to the ground.

Mr. Aschen and I are standing, peering through the tiny window. When one of the prison guards lifts his baton to strike the still-struggling woman, I look away. My counselor does the same.

"You were saying?" I ask.

He looks shaken, deep wrinkles exaggerating every detail of his pained expression. "Nothing. Please, Jacob. Who killed David Bloom?"

"We'll figure it out together. Let me get you closer to another suspect, then. You can't understand this without understanding Emily."

———— ✺ ————

Junior year, Spring

"Slut," one of the blondes said to her friend.

"Whore," her friend responded.

"Skank," came the rebuttal.

They weren't talking to each other, though it might seem that way from a distance. They were talking about Emily, who waited for the bus beside me.

This was a common tactic employed by the vipers. If we fought back, they'd sound their alarms. To teachers, they'd look like the victims, even with their venom in Emily's veins.

But, Emily bent back fangs. She was all dyed black hair and army boots, thick mascara and blood colored lipstick. Lithe, pale frame covered in leather bangles and bracelets, studs and spikes. Most people left the house with varying degrees of comfort and style in mind. Emily? War.

"You know what I look forward to most about my life?" she asked me, tone dripping sarcasm.

"What?"

"Complete lack of responsibility for my future," Emily answered. The two blondes stopped talking. "I can't wait to abandon this token education and latch myself to some successful man, so I can stop being asked to do all this thinking."

"Delightful," I exclaimed. "I hope one day, I can afford to have sex with you."

"At least I can get a man," one of the blondes responded, finally addressing Emily.

Emily only smiled, painted lips curved tightly—bow bent back, ready to fire. She took her time responding, first glancing down at herself. Creamy skin, tight body, all visible through the cigarette burns in her clothes. Looked like something you'd sacrifice a virgin to summon.

"You really don't get it, do you?" Emily asked the snakes. "The joke is on you. You're barely a person; you just do what you're told. The hair, the makeup, the way you dress. It's a script! The music you like, the movies, the way you talk. Just so when you and all your identical friends are lined up at the sorority mixer, you'll have a chance of being bought."

The blonde scoffed, but stayed quiet. Teeth sucked, tongues clucked; both girls retreated, dissatisfied. These girls were nail clippers, and Emily was bolt cutters.

"That's exactly why they don't like you. All that logic," I said.

She hadn't heard. Emily was distracted: she retrieved a vibrating cell phone from the child's lunch-box she used as a purse. "David wants something. Want to come see what it is?"

"How'd you get a phone?" I asked, incredulous.

"I told an old man I would answer when he called. Do you want to come, or not?"

"Yeah, of course." How could I say 'no' to that? "Where is he?"

"Near. C'mon." Emily stood; I followed her, abandoning the bus. We walked around the school, watching the last few teachers escape as evening fell. We crossed the soccer field and ended at the baseball diamond. David stood at the corner of the concession stand, spray paint can in hand, work of art splayed out on the wall before him.

He'd painted an enormous human eye. Underneath this, the words: 'You are who they say you are.'

"What's up?" I asked.

"Bored," he said simply, staring at his handiwork with one hand on his chin. "This isn't doing it for me. I need to break into the office. Are you both okay with that?"

"God, yes," Emily exclaimed. "Give me something to do. What are we waiting for?"

"The office?" I asked. "Do you really think that's a good plan? Aren't there cameras?"

David stared, eyes burning holes through me. "Are you really worried about getting kicked out of school?" he asked. "I mean, what do you plan on doing with your life, Jacob? Wal-Mart greeter? We've got a shot at doing something real here. Who cares what the teachers think?"

A hundred objections came to mind. I might've pointed out David's spotless reputation and how he'd never gotten in trouble, let alone punished. I might've pointed out that my distant future wasn't the concern, but rather the weeks of detention I'd face.

But I didn't. With David standing there, I really only one had option all along. "All right, all right. Let's do this."

We followed David back to the central campus of the school. His lean frame strolled effortlessly across the field, as though he might walk for years and never show fatigue, some natural wanderer.

I held the door open for them; we entered the halls. Eerily calm, after school. Voices ricocheted by, fading echoes—a volleyball team, a choir practice. But mostly, the campus was deserted.

David stopped outside the entrance to the school's office. I glanced up the hallway; no one coming, yet.

Black fingernails wrapped around the doorknob as Emily twisted. Locked.

"Can you pick a lock?" she asked.

"What are you, a secret agent? C'mon." David grinned and pulled a tangled key-chain from his pocket; it jangled noisily. "They lock all the doors, but they don't lock the janitor's closet where they keep the keys. People are unbelievable."

The office door swung slowly open. I was twelve again, on a stolen bike, standing outside a house David broke into.

This time, I didn't make the same mistake, didn't even hesitate. I followed Emily and David inside.

Silence. A familiar pressure, like being underwater. The frantic sensation of trespassing. I froze in my steps, breath coming in rapid gasps as the blood seemed to drain from my head.

My two companions must have been immune. They walked ahead of me, chuckling, pointing at computers, file cabinets and locked desks, speculating what they might hold.

"Not here. We have to go deeper, in the vault," David whispered.

The vault? I didn't dare ask. Didn't want to sound stupid. I followed them past the principals' and nurses' offices to the end of a narrow hallway. At its end: a thick metal door, slightly ajar.

Emily swung open the vault door, holding it open. Rows of filing cabinets greeted us.

"The permanent records," David said, leaning in and taking a big breath of the drawer he'd opened. "The only reason anyone does anything in high school. This file is your whole identity. If you run for office someday, they check your record. Colleges, law schools—they all want to know what's in the file. Your entire identity, as far as that part of the world is concerned. Right here, just open and waiting."

"Make a girl thirsty," Emily mumbled.

David opened another drawer. A column of papers slid out, stacks of neatly divided records. He thumbed through them, chuckling at his findings.

"This is crazy," he said. "We're holding their histories. If I scratch out a line here, make a note there—it'll be a part of who they are. If I put a piece of paper in here that says this guy's dad abused him, everyone will think that's the case. Scared of the color green? Why not. Raised by wolves? Sure."

His finger traced up and down the filing cabinets, searching for a particular record. When he found the cabinet holding his own permanent file, David retrieved the manila folder and pulled the documents out. "I can't believe someone could hold this over me. Why do we let this happen?" The liberator bent the pages in half, then crammed them into his back pocket. These pages were replaced by a folded note that he withdrew from a front pocket.

I stood one cabinet over, skimming through a list of last names, looking for anyone familiar. "What was that?" I asked him. No answer; the file was already replaced and the drawer shut.

Emily held open a folder she'd pulled, apparently hers. "How can one girl have straight A's and still a dozen complaints? Seems unfair. They don't like me." Pouting lips. "Let's start over. Who should I be?" Emily pulled a thick stack of papers from her file and dumped them into the trash. "Not just anyone."

Only half listening, I thumbed through a stack of manila folders. Jamison, Johnson, Joyce. Nora's file. I wondered if she'd ever been in trouble; I opened the folder. Nothing but straight A's and charity work.

Emily's breath rustled the tiny hairs on my neck. "Whatcha got there?" she asked.

"Nothing." I stuffed it back into place.

Wicked nails pinched Nora's file right back out. "Nothing? You look at one file in this whole room, and it's nothing? Then you won't mind if I take some of her good deeds?"

"Don't," I said, regretting it instantly. David turned to look at me. "We're friends," I explained.

"You and Ms. Piggy?" Emily asked, laughing, still holding Nora's file. "Holy crap, look at this: gifted and talented. Accelerated reader. Math Olympics. There's a *Math* Olympics? Are we gonna get drafted into the spelling war? So stupid. This girl has never gotten in trouble in her life." She dug black-painted nails into Nora's identity.

I froze, trapped by my conscience. "Leave it alone," I said. "Anyone else, I don't care. Not her."

Emily's slender hand gripped the file tighter. "And why, precisely, would I do you a favor?"

Could feel David watching as I floundered for an answer.

"I like her," I blurted. "I think. I mean, it's complicated. She's always been nice to me, since eighth grade."

"Let me get this straight: this chubby nerd is more important to you than satisfying a desire that came to me a few seconds ago, completely on a whim?" she asked.

David laughed.

"Yeah, that's what I mean. Sorry, I just—she's been nice to me. Mess with anyone else in the whole school, I don't care."

"Challenge accepted," Emily grinned. She slipped the file back into the drawer. "No problem, anyway."

Close one. When Nora's file was back in the drawer, I shut it and walked over to a black metal box sitting in the far corner of the records room.

"What do you think is in here?" I asked, hoping to change the subject.

David knelt down and tugged at the door; the half-inch sheet of metal swung open. I craned my neck to see over his shoulder. Emily cooed in astonishment.

"The cell phones," she said. "Shiny."

Inside the cabinet were row upon row of confiscated cell phones, each tagged with a student's name and the date they were taken. School policy: if a teacher got mad enough, it'd end up here for a few days.

Many of the phones were identical. Slim black cases and flat glass screens.

"Speaking of identities," Emily said, picking up two of the similar looking phones, "what do you think would happen if we switched around the names, got people the wrong phone? Lots of texts in the memory here, you know? Air the dirty laundry, share the secrets." She pinched one of the plastic labels assigning a name between two fingers and pulled; it peeled away from the case of the phone.

I reached in past her, grabbing one of the devices. So light; cool and metal in my hand. Elegant little piece of science fiction. Should just take it. I deserved it more than them. They owed me, anyway, for all the hell they'd put me through. My hand started to work its way back to my pocket.

"That's not clever," David said.

I put the phone back on the shelf.

A noise came from outside the vault. We tensed, muscles tight. Heard muttering as someone re-locked the office door.

"Let's get out of here," Emily murmured.

15. Poortraits

Junior year

MY PENCIL'S TIP SNAPPED on the tablet of paper in front of me. I'd lost concentration; couldn't stop thinking about breaking into the office. The school seemed different, somehow. Like I knew its secrets.

Last period. Art class sucked—they let us sit in desks and 'express ourselves,' which made me uncomfortable. A lifetime of fending for myself, being left alone—and in the last two years, now that it hardly mattered, everyone seemed interested in Jacob Thorke's feelings.

Adding to that discomfort was Emily, who stood behind me, crowded by easels. I didn't have money for paints, so I'd borrowed a charcoal pencil from the teacher. No idea how Emily conned a cache of colors.

I caught myself staring as she concentrated on the canvas, the end of a brush between full lips. Dark makeup painted over porcelain skin, dewy gaze sunken into deep bruises of eye shadow. The canvas only caught her cast-off. Emily was the real artwork—not only a person, but an image. Emily was *aware*.

The last bell of the day rang. While everyone else filed out of the classroom as quickly as possible, I got stuck trying to give a damn pencil back to a teacher who already stepped out of the room.

"Jacob, would you come and tell me what you think?" Emily asked.

Nervous. Felt my shoulders draw together at the base of my neck. Never knew what to think of Emily, and her chief concern seemed to be making sure this remained true. I went to her, stepping carefully between the easels. Being surrounded by all that amateur artwork made it feel like we were in our own little room.

Her canvas? A random mess of red, black, and yellow.

"It's you," I said.

"Thanks." Didn't know if she took me seriously or not.

"Um...I'm going to get going," I stammered, for lack of anything better to say.

"I wanted to ask you something else."

"Yeah?" Cold sweat forming.

She walked around me, constant dramatist. I turned to pretend to study the painting. Her warm, soft body nestled a little too closely behind mine. The stiff material of a bra shifted against my bicep; a long fingernail traced a line down my spine, coming to rest in my back pocket.

"Have you ever wondered what it would be like? Me and you?" Emily asked. Every consonant pushed hot breath into my ear.

"More than once," I admitted.

"I'd love to find out sometime. Just to experiment, y'know?"

Leg lifted between mine, knee rising up to my crotch gently, feeling the results of her work. Then, a hand on the side of my face. Couldn't even feel her skin, only the rush of the fact it was happening. Emily pulled me into her, other hand squeezing me. "Tag."

Fifteen minutes to do something life changing.

Our lips met. Her tongue slipped wetly below mine. Emily's hand went up into the air; I didn't know why.

I heard a grunt of disgust and sensed motion in the doorway. I looked up to see a girl walking away.

"Thanks for coming, Nora," Emily called to her.

Dread wrapped cold fingers around my heart and squeezed. I pulled away from Emily, took two steps back, then weaved through the easels toward the door.

"Let her go. Jesus," Emily said to me.

Needed to find Nora. It's not like we were dating, not sure why I cared so much—but I knew I should.

Must mean something.

I turned into the hallway. Nora stopped, turned and watched me approach.

"Sorry I interrupted," she said, speech tight, eyes wet. "I should have known that Emily..." her voice cracked. She tried to speak again but failed, and put a hand up to her face instead.

"Emily is messing with you. With us. She thinks I like you, Nora. I mean, *I* think I like you, too."

Nora stared at the ground, refusing eye contact. She tried to speak, but her voice cracked again. Finally: "Looks like you like Emily."

"Emily and I are friends, Nora. She only kissed me to mess with me. I didn't even know you liked me, come on. I'm a joke in this school. And, I don't want to be with Emily. She's...Emily is crazy, Nora. I couldn't date her if I tried, believe me. She's just messing with me."

"*If you tried?*" Nora sniffed back tears. I sensed the tide changing. "So let me get this straight: you were just kissing, and you've *tried* to date her—but you'd still settle for me. Gee, thanks. Forget it, Jacob." She spun and marched out of the school, leaving me dumbfounded, gripping my forehead and looking back and forth between the art room and the school's exit.

Emily approached. "You should've let me take her file."

"Seriously? Is that why you did all this?"

She shrugged, grinning. "C'mon, it's obvious she likes you. Since the file clearly defines the person...If I had her file, maybe I'd like you, too."

"What do you care? Are you asking me out?"

Emily laughed. "I don't have boyfriends, Jacob."

"Then why do you care if I have a girlfriend?"

"Because you're mine." She bit her lip to kill the smile growing there.

16. David graduates

Now

"**I** BARELY TALKED TO NORA for the rest of the year," I say. "Some friends, right? I'll never understand women. Why couldn't Nora have told me she was interested earlier?"

Mr. Aschen looks at me, clearly unimpressed. "Jacob, problems with girls are perfectly normal at your age. What's not normal is, y'know—the cult, the unwavering devotion to a sociopath, the illegal activity. Let's try and focus on what got you arrested."

"You call him a sociopath, but you're wrong," I argue.

"It's absolutely correct: David was a complete narcissist. In his mind, he was the only human on a planet full of apes. Maybe I shouldn't speak ill of the dead, but we need to focus on *you* now. There's nothing we can do for David," Mr. Aschen says, hands holding a piece of paper drawn from the manila folder.

"You're lying." My voice is louder than expected. Maybe I care more than I want to admit. "David wasn't an egomaniac, and I'm not some trained monkey. He led through example. No one was more serious about Eureka than David—look at everything he sacrificed."

"You're talking about graduation. I'm familiar with it, but please —tell me, Jacob. Tell me what's so great about this particular tragedy." Now the pen is in his hand, ready to write.

Junior year, last day

I still spoke with Nora a few times after Emily's ambush, but things weren't the same. More than kissing Emily, too—there was a larger disconnect between us. Eureka made a wide divide.

But even Eureka's fate was in jeopardy: today, David graduated, presumably leaving Kingwood forever. Scholarships came easy for a low income guy with a hundred and four point three GPA. He could go where he wanted.

And what would my life be, then? No Eureka, no break-ins, no excitement. I needed David to stay, but I couldn't tell him. All I could do was watch him graduate, and pretend to be happy.

Half the city lined up in the stands of the Kingwood coliseum. Red and white striped paper bags of popcorn, thick pickles in plastic baggies. Little brothers and sisters watching, wedged between mom and dad. A badly-tuned marching band in full regalia, on the bleachers opposite me, rampaged through a rendition of the school song. A dark fist of storm clouds gathered far on the horizon; several knobby cumulus knuckles threatened to unfurl into raking sheets of rain.

Most of the Six sat in the bleachers near me. The public event would make a devastating place for a tag—and everyone seemed to understand that, so tensions ran high. By my count, Steven was 'it.' I kept constant track of him; he sat on the bottom row.

Kent and Cameron sat together, up above me, watching the proceedings. While the spectators continued to trickle in, the seniors stood fidgeting outside. David stood at the head of the procession.

The sound of trumpets retuning called the hair on the back of my neck to attention. Moments later, the march began. The long line of seniors moved to the front of the field, where they'd be displayed before taking their seats for the rest of the ceremony. As they crossed the area in front of the crowd, teachers and friends stood in a line to congratulate them. Happy Kingwood bullshit.

I scanned the faces of the attendees and caught one snag in the otherwise smooth procession: Steven, glasses gleaming, waiting for David to pass him.

Gotta get down there. If Steven tagged David now—I didn't want to guess what would happen. Too much. I ran down the bleachers, working to wedge my way through the crowd. Soon, though, the bodies got too thick; even when I tugged at the shoulder in front of me, it didn't budge.

The line of graduating seniors advanced slowly, each shuffling step bringing David closer to Steven. Slow-motion train wreck. The two friends stood a few feet apart. I was ten feet away, trapped.

David could turn back. He could just avoid him, walk around. I would have.

They met. Steven shook the older boy's hand, then reached out and clapped David on the back. I didn't need to be able to read lips to tell the single syllable spoken.

Felt my heart stop, restart, then stop again. Now what?

If David was worried to only have fifteen minutes to change his life in front of the entire town, it didn't show. After another round of applause for the seniors, they took seats on the field. The principal stepped up to a podium to begin the introductions. After a bit of sentimental nonsense, the administrator announced my friend:

"And now we present your valedictorian, David Bloom," a low voice boomed out from the dozen stacked speakers.

Thunderous ovation. And why not? Kid from the wrong part of town who beat all the odds, had the highest grades in his class. David stood, looking shocked and amazed, humble as always.

I couldn't help but ride a swell of pride.

David cleared his throat, and the audience fell still. "Thank you for this honor," he began, then stopped and looked around.

I tried to imagine myself in his shoes, with minutes left to complete the tag. Would he ignore Steven's challenge and graduate like normal? That'd be my reaction. But, I knew from experience: David didn't compromise.

He spoke: "I thought a long time about what I'd say up here today. I've been a victim of Kingwood my whole life." A nervous titter from the audience. "I'm from another part of town. A little circle of trailers, in the woods, called Broadway. It was made clear to me early on that we lived in two different worlds, that I was an outsider. It's okay, though. I'm good at fitting in." David smiled, stepped back from the microphone and shook his head before leaning in. "A part of being on the outside is noticing things. I've noticed that the system is broken. Hell, I didn't help things—but it was broken a long time before I cheated my way to being valedictorian."

You couldn't manufacture this kind of silence.

"The way our grades are decided is a joke. We're ranked and ordered by how well we can manipulate the system. Take the right classes, with the right teachers. It has almost nothing to do with learning. I decided to take advantage of that—I organized with about forty of the seniors sitting behind me in those little metal chairs. We all cheated our way to the top, sharing tests and homework. None of them thought I'd announce this today, but it's time to put a bullet in the head of a structure that's been broken for too long. You've all been cheated; the class rankings are a lie. Anyway, sorry in advance for the trouble this will cause. It's been real. Thank you."

Silence reigned. The spectators sat, mouths slack, as parents and students tried sucking in air to cool overheating brains.

The first sound was someone trying to start a slow clap. It failed.

The second sound? One of David's teachers breaking into tears.

The third was everyone shifting uncomfortably in their seats.

David walked straight off the field. A dirty little murmur metastasized into to an argument within the crowd: was it true? The results of the entire year were now in question.

The ground dropped from under me; I'd never expected our game to go this far. David Bloom forfeited his own future, his scholarships—and for what? To make a statement. To piss people off. All because of Eureka.

And Steven was responsible. The little shit; he should've known better. He should've known David couldn't say no.

Steven began working his way through the crowd. Something in the way he smiled boiled my blood. Not anger: *rage.* An uncontrollable urge to beat the crap out of this smug little punk. Steven thought he'd done something amazing.

I wondered about taking the fall for him with Kent. Did he plan that, too? Was he really hurting, or did he just know I was a sucker for guilt trips—that I'd do anything to keep everyone friends?

The little nerd retreated back under the bleachers. I followed closely, pushing my way past the slow-moving line of confused audience members. Steven's shoulder was in reach; I grabbed on and spun him to face me. I tried to say something, but the words wouldn't come.

Then he aimed the smirk at me. I couldn't handle it; I shoved him, hard, sending him tripping over an older man in a suit and tie.

Steven charged back at me, fist connecting with my cheek. Hit a lot harder than I thought he would; the immediate numbness evolved into burning pain. I punched him back. Steven tackled me, arms wrapped around my knees, dragging me down. We rolled around, swinging at each other, each working to pin the other.

Graduation was over.

As I fought to stand, bodies collided with Steven's then mine, sending me rolling back into the cement. Someone in a blue uniform grappled with my hands, which I kept extended, desperately warding away whatever was coming.

Pepper spray hissed. May as well have been a flamethrower. My eyes, cheeks and mouth ignited in blinding pain. Logic left me; I kept swinging.

I felt my hand connect with something, then focused enough to see a police officer clutching his jaw, looking shocked.

Punched a cop. I stopped fighting, before someone shot me.

A second set of arms rolled me over then forced my arms back before a knee was planted on my spine. I rubbed my flaming face into the cool concrete, realizing handcuffs now restrained me. A moment later, I was lifted to a standing position and marched off the field. A kind of reverse graduation, really.

They put me in the back of a police cruiser. Glad to be out of the public eye. I propped up against the seat and waited, crying out the pepper spray. I didn't want to go to jail.

The next few hours passed in stop-motion; I remembered individual frames of activity but none of it felt real, felt connected. The police had me, first—the principal talked them out of an arrest. They dropped me off at the school, on a Saturday.

The principal was pissed. More at David than us, I think, but David wasn't in his office. No one knew where he was, apparently.

I didn't really care. I was emotionally dead, just staggering through the day.

Steven went first; I'd sat and listened through the door as I waited in small chair outside. Dreading my turn. The principal's voice modulations were a good sign of how angry he was; each line of low whispers was punctuated by a roaring finale.

When it was my turn to sit in the single chair at the opposite end of the administrator's desk, he didn't speak for a long time. I studied the poster of Lincoln behind him, counted the leaves on the small fern in the corner. The phone sat disconnected on his desk, little plug dangling uselessly off the side of the table.

After several minutes, he spoke. "Why are you incapable of behaving decently in public?"

Because I grew up in a trailer park, sir. Because I have no mother, sir. And so it went. I nodded when necessary, waiting in the corner of my own mind for this ordeal to pass.

Somewhere in the litany of lectures and threats, the principal made a comment. "I tried to check his file. David's, I mean, to see if he was disturbed or something. You know what I found? One page. One goddamn page." Red-faced, lights on his ceiling reflected on the bald circle of his scalp.

"What do you mean?" I asked.

He dug into a desk drawer and pulled out a single sheet. Plain white copy paper, marred with two words: all caps, bold, underlined.

David Bloom.

"This is what's in David's permanent record. Makes us look like idiots." He put a hand to his beet-red forehead, then plugged the cord into his phone. It rang immediately; he picked up the receiver and slammed it down. "I'm going to take some phone calls. You stay here. I'm not done with you. Wait in the hall."

He led me outside his office. I took a seat next to Steven, waiting for the next round.

My fury at Steven lay cold. I was still pissed at him—but I'd punched him, repeatedly, and had no other way to express my anger. Because I'd done all I could, my mind seemed to reset itself, and we fell back into our old ways.

"What'd you get?" I asked him.

"They tried to give me long-term detention. No thanks," he answered. "I'm dropping out of school. They can kiss my ass."

"Bold. I got long-term, too."

"I'm making ten grand a year now, fixing computers. I can double that if I don't have school. I'll get my GED and move out of the foster center; I'd rather do that than go to detention. Wouldn't you?"

"I guess," I said. "What about David, where is he staying?"

"Not in foster care, I can tell you that. They've pretty much given up looking for him. He used to disappear every other weekend, then every other night. Now, I never see him."

"I need to talk to him," I said. "Make sure he's all right."

Steven was silent for a moment. "I think I'm going to quit."

"What? Why?"

He looked down at the gray tile floor. "What's next for Eureka? Do I need to do something like that? No way. I'm not throwing away everything for some game."

"So why'd you tag him, then?"

Steven stared at the ground. His glasses sat crooked, bent from my fists.

"Wait," I said, "were you hoping David would back out? That's it, right? You thought tagging him during the valedictorian's speech would make him quit."

"I just wanted to know. David is great, don't get me wrong. But...I mean, come on. Would you do what he just did? Would you throw it all away for a game?"

"Let me get this straight—you tried to call his bluff?" I asked.

"Yeah."

"And it didn't work?" I pressed.

"Yeah."

"And now you're quitting?"

Steven sighed, palms in the air. "If this is what Eureka is, if that's what it takes to be David's friend, I'm not sure I want to do that. If I keep playing, whatever I do next will have to be better than what David did. So, what do I do? Shoot myself in the head? That'd change things."

I shook my head, disgusted, and didn't say anything else. In truth, I hadn't worked out all my own feelings about what happened, either.

The principle opened the door. The rest of the day passed in a blur. Endless lectures. I could tell from the onset, this was serious.

The administrator was furious. I tried to argue out of my sentence, but they wouldn't budge. My fate was sealed: for senior year I'd be in long-term detention. The 'bad kids' school. Probably where I belonged, anyway.

17. The talented Mr. Bloom

I IMAGINE SOME PARENTS would've grounded their kids, or taken away their privileges. But, my dad seemed convinced he didn't have any kind of control over me. Instead, he simply condemned me wholesale, and seemed to write me off as a lost cause. By the end of the first week of summer, we just stopped talking.

As to what happened to David—I still didn't know what to think. David was a hero, but Steven should've known better. Why would Steven be so desperate to push his buttons? If David was a pyromaniac, would Steven hand him a lighter? We had to play the game within reason, right? Otherwise we'd all end up in jail.

The Broadway plot where David's trailer sat was empty. The grass was dead in a big rectangle where the home rested all those years; a trail of trampled lawn led toward the woods.

Tire tracks led me through the forest. I followed the impressions until they ended at a small clearing, nearly half a mile into the wild lands.

David's trailer sat beneath an oak, dingy and yellowed, windows cracked and wheels flat. His laundry was strung up on a long line connecting to a neighboring tree. In addition to the flannel shirts and worn jeans, a single black bra hung from the clothes line. *Go David.*

I paused outside and took a deep breath before knocking on the door. A moment later, he answered, smiling down at me.

"Hey," he said, stepping back so I could enter.

Paintings lined the walls of the narrow trailer; explosive splashes of color. Some of the oils still looked wet. I tried to ignore the artwork—didn't want to seem overly impressed.

"What brings you by?" David wasn't surprised by the visit, which wasn't surprising.

"I haven't talked to you in a while, is all," I said. "Wanted to see what you were up to out here. Broadway is kinda lonely without you."

He turned to face one of the paintings. "Foster care made me realize I'd rather be alone. Easier to live this way, even if it's in Mom's old trailer."

"How's your mom doing, anyway?"

"She's dead," he said simply.

"I'm sorry." A silence settled.

Everything in the trailer was yellow with age; the windows were open and it was humid inside, so much that my breath felt wet. A pair of thick spectacles sat on a small kitchen table which jutted from the wall, glass lenses cataract with scratches. An old design, big teardrop frames made of metal, bent from sitting uneven all those years.

I tried to revive the conversation: "So, did you paint these, or what?" Three colorful canvases covered the available space in the mobile home. They were composed of lines and colors which didn't seem to signify anything in particular, yet all had some untraceable common theme.

"Yeah. Have a seat," he said, smiling. "Want some water or something?"

"I'm fine, thanks." I sat down on a cushioned platform.

"They're music," David said.

"What?"

"The paintings. I draw music. Usually other people's songs, but I've started to compose, too. See? This one is Beethoven, the fourth movement of the Ninth Symphony."

The painting ran in a linear fashion from left to right, with the left half made of foreboding shades of blue and gray. Large, thick black and red lines consumed the right half, the climax. Graceful swirls of color, just like the song.

"That one is old. Here's a newer one—the 1812 Overture."

This painting did not seem linear, but rather a summation of the entire song. Soft cascades of fingerprints laid out the gentle rise of violins, until the piece erupted into burnt orange and brown holes like cigarette burns. Jagged lines across the top of the painting presented the ferocious melody. Giant black polka dots along the bottom, perfect circles, were the bass. While I looked at the painting, I could almost hear the song.

"This one is an original," he said, motioning to a different canvas.

This one was circular, but made sense; the image *felt* like a song. Abstract, but it clicked somehow, musically.

"I'm impressed. I can *hear* them."

David smiled again. "Good. That's the idea."

"So is this what you do now? Paint?"

"I've been trying new things, lately."

"I noticed." I paused, unable to hold back the question burning through my brain, then blurted: "So, did you really cheat?"

He laughed, stuffed hands in pockets, slouched his shoulders. "No. Just wanted to give them a kick in the ass on my way out, you know. Only had fifteen minutes to come up with that."

"Don't you regret it, though? You had scholarships, college and everything. I mean, can you still go?"

"What if I told you something I've never told anyone before?" he asked.

"Tell me."

"I don't feel anything," David said, leaning forward as he did so, lock of hair falling in front of his right eye.

I stared ahead, unable to speak for a moment. Then: "What?"

"I don't feel feelings, not like other people do. There's just nothing there. When we broke into the school office, you were terrified—I could see it on your face. I didn't feel anything. When my mother died, nothing. Not since I was very young. So when you ask me if I regret what I did at graduation, that question is kind of lost on me."

"You don't have *feelings?*"

"Not as such." He said this matter-of-factly, like explaining math to a child. "I'm not some monster. I have a code I live by, and I don't mean to harm people. But I think people are harming themselves, and Eureka can help with that. You should know—you were the first person to realize what it could be. I didn't understand the effect it has on normal people, I mean people with feelings, until you showed me. It forces people to embrace the thing they fear most, the same thing that makes up the realness of life. Change. Think of every abused wife who sticks with her husband because she doesn't see any way out for herself. Think of everyone stuck at a miserable desk job, rotting from the inside out. People who are paralyzed by life—nearly everyone. People stuck to their pasts, to their possessions, to their relationships, and all they need is permission to change."

"I've seen the same things," I admitted. "I'm just worried about this going too far."

"You're right to be concerned. Because of my predicament—with my feelings, or lack thereof—I have to be very aware of myself. Being careful doesn't come naturally to me, I find, because I don't know when I am supposed to be scared. But you always have, and you've always been there to warn me. Remember when we broke into that house? You told me to stop. You were right; that got out of hand. I should have listened. People seem to get hurt when I ignore your advice."

"I didn't do much good during graduation," I countered. "You didn't ask me."

"I'm asking you now. I'm 'it,' right? What if I let you decide? What if I let you hold onto it, and then you'll be able to tell me—is this right? And if you never tag anyone, well then, I guess that'll be my answer. But I mean this, Jacob. I'm giving you something very important. This is *me.*"

"You'd trust me like that?"

"I know what you'll choose," David said. His hand rested on my forearm. "You don't have to change right now; I want you to decide if it's the right thing to do, first. But, you're 'it' now."

That day, David left the future of Eureka in my hands—and I wasn't sure what to do with it.

18. High hopes

Now

I LOOK MR. ASCHEN IN THE EYE. "Can't you see? David trusted me. He gave me the power to decide what would happen. How could he have been using me, if I had control?"

"Those are only words, Jacob. He only told you something to make you feel important. He's a manipulator. How did this end? Did you get to decide Eureka's fate? You have to look past the words. You have to look at the numbers, at the math. The math doesn't lie."

I lean back in my chair. If I try, I can reach the opposite end of the room with my foot. I don't want to answer this part.

Mr. Aschen sighs and folds the manila envelope closed. "Do you mind if I ask you a somewhat petty question, Jacob?"

I cross my arms. "That's all we're doing here, right?"

"Why did you stop coming to counseling sessions with me?"

"You don't need counseling when you've got Eureka," I tell him.

"Did David tell you that?"

Well, not directly. I don't answer this, either.

Mr. Aschen puts the black and silver pen into his shirt pocket and folds his hands, all graying dignity. "I only ask because I stopped doing volunteer work when you stopped coming to our sessions. I was a bit disappointed to learn David was a suitable replacement for me. Well, not suitable, obviously."

"Not David. Jesus, Mr. Aschen, I keep trying to get this across to you. It's not all about David. It's Eureka. The idea might have come from anywhere. You just keep bringing up David because you think I'll say I secretly hated him, that I killed him. I didn't."

Mr. Aschen only raises an eyebrow and grins again, like a poker player who's confident in his hand. "You found me out. But, really—I miss our sessions. This may be bad of me to say, but I never managed to connect with the others in your *gang*." The aging psychologist emphasizes the word. "You've always been my favorite. I think you have the most potential, even more than David." He speaks into his folded fingers.

"Now you're the one who's manipulating. Isn't it bad form to pick favorites?"

"They aren't my clients anymore," Mr. Aschen informs me. "Society failed you, Jacob. You and your friends have been mistreated. But, out of the whole sad mess of Broadway Trailer Park, you're the one I thought I had the most hope of reaching. Unfortunately, David took the opportunity from me. You can't see it, Jacob, but you're infatuated with him. He's the only male role model you've ever had, and you've come to think of him as your father figure."

Denial springs eternal. "Let me just tell you what happened next, all right?"

Senior year, August

Late during the summer, I finally got a bit of good luck: Dad got arrested for drunk driving. With his license revoked, he couldn't drive for the next year. I had to take him to his community service, to the corner store and back—but out of necessity, I got the car.

Had to suffer some awkward conversations. Counted every stitch on the steering wheel during the red lights. He was not happy about my getting sent to long term. I think for him, this signaled some sort of change in me. I was on the wrong path, officially. At least I wasn't drunk-driving down it.

Still. A car.

Although—my car wasn't like other cars. Other cars guzzled gasoline and belched black smoke that blazed holes in the ozone.

My car, on the other hand, sipped petrol with a pinky in the air and covered its mouth when it coughed. It started like a suspicious lump and stopped like a slow death.

I drove my little blue box up to the long-term detention parking lot and took a deep breath. My first day. I resisted the urge drive away from—hell, maybe *through*—the school.

The sign out front read 'Hope High School.' As in, 'I hope you'll be tried as adults.'

The first day of school, and Hope High was silent. Students walked listlessly, feet dragging, staring blankly ahead. I thought they'd at least see a friend, get excited—but, no. Like summer never happened; this could have been any day of the year. No one made eye contact.

Seemed like everyone around me had been there forever.

I made my way to my first—and only—classroom, and sat down in the back. The moment my ass connected to the chair, time began slipping by, out of my grasp. The first day became the first week, just like the next, and the one before it. Apathy nation. Everyone cared so little and talked so seldom; I lived in the personification of the word *whatever*. The vocabulary was as slim as...it sucked. It sucked, was all.

Something about it lulled me into a kind of gray state of being, where the passage of time slipped by meaninglessly.

The 'teachers' acted more like babysitters, and keeping riot level pandemonium to a minimum seemed to be good enough for them. Like they knew the students stood on a keen edge, and given the right circumstances, might actually have an emotion about something.

But, the staff seemed to understand the one thing keeping them from being locked into closets and the school from being burnt down was the fact no one *cared* about being screwed over. As long as the students didn't care, they were fine. And it was easy to not care, really. Every day was exactly the same; blink your eyes and another week was gone. Nothing happened worth remembering.

Funny, that.

The school work we 'bad kids' were given consisted of a giant pile of homework from our collective classes, if the teachers even remembered to send it. With no directions or assistance, the assignments were best used as projectiles.

As for the students, well, it wasn't exactly like Kingwood High. This place was temporary, and you were pretty likely to meet someone who would punch you for no reason. Friends were rare.

My first month, I talked to one guy—the guy who looked most like me. Geoff Harper. His shirt read *I can't believe I shaved my balls for this,* and he smelled so much like weed, I thought he somehow constructed a bong out of his own body.

We'd said five or six things to each other. Getting right along.

Geoff turned to me; I made sure to be cool enough not to notice. "I hate this place. Let's get stoned." He flashed a tightly rolled joint from beneath the desk, out of the teacher's view.

My life wasn't going at all like I'd planned. I wanted to be in school—in *normal* school, with Nora and my friends. David gave me an important assignment, and I needed them. If I was going to tag someone, it wouldn't happen here.

So, every day at lunch, I'd sneak off with Geoff and get high. Certainly helped to pass the time. When your whole life is shit, well...sometimes you have to make your own fun.

"Whenever homeless people ask me for money," Geoff said as he lit the joint, "I tell them I would love to help, but I am a Scientologist, and it's against my religion to give to the needy."

"Why do you not want to give money to homeless people? It's just change, man," I said, inhaling a thick, hot stream of smoke. "Don't be greedy."

"That's not why," Geoff said. "I just hate Scientologists."

Getting to know Geoff confirmed what I suspected from the moment I met him: he was like me. His parents split up and neither wanted much to do with him; my new friend lived off the good will of a relatively wealthy uncle. As such, Geoff had his own place. The apartment was a total dump, but being there made me feel like a king. We drank beer and smoked in safety.

Before long, being his friend made life at Hope High something I might even survive.

We made a habit out of getting high together pretty often. *Screw it*, I figured. *I'm already in the bad kid's school. Might as well be one.*

Something insidious about it all. What was happening to me? It was stupid, I knew. Not stupid to be doing what I was doing, getting high—that was just making the best of my boring situation. But the whole place was under this cloud of ease, of laziness. No challenge, no expectations. Hope High was a holding pen, purgatory for the hopeless. I was adrift in the mundane.

19. Virgins

Now

---❦---

"YOU'RE AVOIDING MY QUESTION, JACOB," Mr. Aschen says. "You still haven't answered–what happened with David? Did he really let you decide his fate?"

I sigh.

---❦---

Senior year, October

Weeks passed in a fuzzy yellow haze. Or, they must have, because I was there when it happened–or so I'm told. My witnesses, however, were unreliable.

I'm not gonna lie; David was pretty much out of mind. Not on purpose, but–just trying to survive. Without the Six, without Eureka, things got stagnant. No reason to try. The slippery slope of the stupid.

To make matters worse, I never saw the Six. So for a minute one Monday morning, I witnessed a bit of truth–truth so surprising, I wasn't sure if it was real or a hallucination. Always my trouble with the truth.

It started as a peculiar sensation of being watched while I crossed the parking lot. I turned to glimpse a familiar presence, partially obscured by giant movie starlet sunglasses and ribbons of long, dark hair. A girl in black dress, with a face I'd assumed was done with me. A face that brought me nothing but trouble.

Seeing her made me think again; made me care. Did being 'it' matter? Did anyone still want to play? And if so, did they want anything to do with me?

So I turned around and kept walking across the parking lot. Been lying so long, I forgot what the truth was, really.

The next day, the eyes watched me again.

On the third day, a note on my car read: *Help me.*

On the fourth day, I searched for her and she was gone.

On the fifth day, I walked up behind her car and tapped on the glass, trying to scare her. That didn't work, so I just sat down in Emily's passenger seat and asked what she wanted.

"I want you, of course," Emily said. "I need your help."

"I thought you were in school."

She giggled. "I am. Don't look at me like that, Mr. Miscreant, like you're one to judge. Are you *high*? Jesus, that's new."

"Yeah, well, things change." I leaned back and put my feet on the dash.

"That's the name of the game. Speaking of which..." Emily put her car in gear and started driving away from the school.

"Wait up," I said. "I need to be in class. They'll call my dad."

"Too bad," she said with a smile. "I want you to get me high. I've never been high."

No point in complaining; she was going to get her way, and it'd just make me look weak. "Turn right here." I directed us to a familiar waterfall, a place I'd discovered while exploring with the Six.

"I'm bored," she said. "And I don't mean like, I can't think of anything to do. I mean, like, this chronic, soul-crushing boredom. It won't leave me alone. Just want to bash my head into walls, Jacob. Every day for the foreseeable future looks exactly the same. My life just...doesn't feel *right.*"

"Yeah? How?"

"School, this, everything." She took her hands off the wheel and motioned around the car. "It's just so—I don't know. What's the point? I can see my future, Jacob."

"See your future?"

"Yeah. It's laid out flat. You know...college, get a degree, get a job, get a car, get a house, work, get married, make babies, die. Right? But I don't want that. I don't want anything like that."

"That's the way life's supposed to work."

"And that's like—the best possible outcome! Christ. I've missed you. Things aren't the same. No one will ever see me like David does, like you all do." She took a deep breath. "And look at you," she continued. "You're doing great." No sarcasm. "You don't give a shit about what anyone thinks, do you? You do your own thing. Sexy. Plus, I know a secret." She pressed her lips together and grinned. A hand snaked up the back of my neck; long fingernails raked over my scalp, sending ripples of pleasure down my arms and legs.

We stopped at my favorite spot, a secluded little patch of land on the corner of a farmer's property. *'Private Property'* signs were posted everywhere, but I'd never seen another human being here. The waterfall stood short and fat, ten feet of channeled water.

We got out of the car and walked over to a rocky embankment next to the pond where the falls emptied. I pulled the tiny metal pipe and bag of weed from the side of my shoe and sat on a large, flat rock. She sat across from me and we took turns puffing out of the pipe, sucking down deep breaths of acrid smoke.

Emily was new to this. She coughed on her first time, like everyone did—the giggles started soon after.

Strange, being more experienced at something than Emily. She'd always been a step ahead of me, always been able to screw with me, embarrass me, and tease me. For once, our positions got reversed.

"So, you mentioned a secret?" I asked.

"Oh, c'mon. I know David tagged you. This isn't fair. You can't...you can't keep Eureka to yourself. You gotta let us play, Jacob."

But, hadn't David left me to decide?

"Do you want to?"

"Yeah, I want to. I'm here, aren't I?" She giggled.

Could taste her lipstick on the pipe. I put the weed away before she got too far gone to talk.

Emily slid forward, crawling across the rock we shared until she sat beside me. My nervous system scrambled from the pinprick sensations of long hair brushing against my arm.

She didn't stop coming closer. An arm slid over my body, so that Emily lay across my lap, looking up at me. Lips came close; her thin tongue slipped from between them, playfully licking mine. "This 'tagging' thing, it's for kids," she whispered, reaching into her purse and presenting a condom. "How about we try something a little more intimate? I'd say I still get to be 'it.'"

I was a virgin, though not for lack of trying. And here was Emily, offering herself to me for no particular reason.

My pulse pounded on my eardrums. I leaned forward, touched her lips with mine. She smiled; I felt it through my lips, like dancers and hips. We kissed.

This couldn't be real. It seemed so forced, so planned. Okay, yeah, I wanted to sleep with her. Who wouldn't? But this was too fast; I needed time to think. My body was a quivering mess.

She moved in, kissed again—harder. I pulled my mouth away from her sucking grasp. "What's really happening here? I haven't seen you in forever."

Emily leaned back, nonplussed. "I just don't fucking like it. No one knows me, all right? No one is playing Eureka, no one cares, and worse—I don't care. About anything. Make me care, Jacob. Save me from this boredom."

A strong wind blew across the mundane. We were moving again.

She giggled again and tilted forward. Our lips almost touched; we hovered an atom's width apart. She was waiting for my decision.

I leaned forward and kissed her, hard. "Tag," I mouthed into her lips.

Emily's fingers curled into my hair, pulling me down until I lay flat and watched the clouds above. She climbed on top of me; warm thighs gripped my bare stomach.

Something voyeuristic about doing this in the middle of the day on the farmer's private property. No one around for miles, and we'd hear any cars coming. The sun shone close, breathing down our necks. My skin burned; sweat dripped down my forehead.

Emily seemed intent on giving the birds a show, lifting her dress and tossing it aside, revealing milky, pale skin and a black lace bra, which dropped next.

Probably not her first time. I tried to pretend it wasn't mine.

Emily attacked me with hungry hands and a thirsty mouth. Biting, licking, scratching, clawing, sucking. At least half of it felt good. She seemed to be on some recorded track, like she knew to do this for five minutes, then that, as though a director gave instruction as he filmed us. I suspected she'd done a lot of video research.

My senses were alight. The sun seemed to sear the surface of my brain; every sensation registered raw and real.

As she ripped my last article of clothing away, my last shield against her, passion overtook me, and I wanted to do anything to make her feel good. I might swallow her whole if she'd let me.

And for those moments, I loved Emily. Loved her in the way that included my genuine dislike of her. During the act, emotions sprung up in me I knew didn't belong. For some reason, I wanted to convince her somehow, she might be loved—I might fix her.

I, Jacob Thorke, wanted to help someone. Not only help her—save her.

Emily enthralled. Mouth open, deep panting breaths, hair splayed wildly, rogue strands shining like beams of light in the sun. All warm mouths, awkward fumbling, tight places.

Afterward, when we lay naked and panted to catch our breath, sharing a cigarette and wondering how we would act after we got back in the car—this was when I started thinking again.

The warmth left me. Noble notions of saving Emily and the unimpeachable cache of mercy and love were floating down the stream in a condom. For a moment, it seemed I might have made something magical out of a barren situation.

When we finished, things had changed. I *knew* her; witnessed some part of her that was forbidden. Emily wasn't as cool as I thought she was; not as invincible as she pretended to be. The way the pale-skinned beauty got dressed again, avoiding eye contact, seeming to shrink within her own body. Suddenly, Emily was *real*. An actual girl with insecurities and vulnerabilities. Not just a living piece of performance art.

Should I feel guilty? But, who used whom?

I prepared to comfort her, but she spoke first. "Thanks. You're no David, of course, but that wasn't totally bad."

Gut punch. I stared into the water. Of course—she wouldn't have sex with me if she wasn't going to ruin it by telling me she'd also had sex with David, and he was better.

"Don't make this weird," she said, lighting another cigarette. "It's about the game, that's all."

All that passion, gone—now, just cold water. Numb. Then again, what had I expected? To have a relationship with Emily? Movie dates and walks on the beach?

Even more troubling—what drove Emily to seek me out? To sleep with me? How much was David involved? At that moment, I could blame the death of David Bloom on my inferiority complex.

20. Hate in healthy doses

Now

"How devoted to David was Emily?" Mr. Aschen asks.

"No idea," I say tonelessly. "She was having sex with him. Hell, David might've been the only person on Earth Emily didn't act superior to."

"So when you say David let you decide the fate of Eureka, did he really? Or did he ask Emily to make sure you tagged someone, knowing you had feelings for her?"

I press my lips together. Not my favorite thought: could Emily be so shallow she'd take my virginity because David asked?

"There's more to the story, though. Let's talk about what led to his death. Let's talk about Eureka."

"I have a very hard time wrapping my mind around the game. I can't think of a single reason to go along with David's experiment, other than to impress David." He leans forward, elbows on knees. "It seems like Eureka makes you give up the things that make life worth living—a family, romance, a job, building a foundation! Those are the things I treasure in life, Jacob. I just can't..." Mr. Aschen holds his chin in a gnarled hand, skin like bark. "Personally, I think Eureka is a tool David used to earn your devotion. The game unbalances you, makes you look for direction."

"I disagree. Eureka was easy to start playing," I explain. "You get *one turn* at life, and you're more or less assigned a role from the start. Some people get a pretty nice life. We got a bad one. But, the idea should be true for anyone. If this is your one opportunity at life, isn't the ultimate homage you can pay to God, or even to yourself, to explore every facet of life? Isn't that a nobler ideal than raising a family? There are plenty of families. Maybe if you live in a time or a place where life *means* something, where you're fighting in a war or rebuilding after one, or *something* with some narrative... but here in America, here and now, life has no point for us. So why not do the best thing possible, and just explore?

"Could everyone play Eureka? No, society wouldn't function. But should everyone who *can* play Eureka, do so? I don't know. I don't know. But me and mine, much as I can hate them, I know: we are the result of all this *quality of life* that has taken the place of the actual quality of your life. But, you do have some parts right—you have to be a little selfish to play Eureka. You have to be willing to disappoint the people around you, because that's part of breaking their hold on you. So, maybe I'm a sociopath, or a narcissist, or whatever you said David was."

Mr. Aschen leans back, shoulder against the wall. He leafs through the manila folder of notes, perhaps looking for inspiration to launch a counterattack. After a moment of staring at nothing in particular, he lurches forward.

"Nothing is wrong with you, Jacob. You care about other people, no matter how hard you try to deny the fact. You're a healthy, normal, intelligent young man. If anything, out of your whole crew of misfits, you care most—and they used that against you. You're looking for acceptance, and David managed to convince you he was the only one who should provide it. You're a smart kid. I can't understand why you don't apply the same intelligence to look at your life objectively and see David controlled you. Look past the narrative—look at the math. The numbers don't lie. At the end of the day, you're still here defending David, after everything that went wrong, even though he's dead. You're here, under arrest, facing prison, and out of some sort of loyalty to him, you won't tell us what happened."

"I'm telling you what happened. David died because we started playing Eureka again. After I tagged Emily, she tagged someone else."

Senior year, October

I sat inside our small trailer and flipped across the six channels we got through an aluminum-foil-enhanced antennae. Nothing but sports, which I didn't like. Why did they have to keep competing every year? Couldn't they just figure out who the winners were, and call it quits?

I was lost. Emily pulled me out of the mundane just long enough to take what she needed, and then she dropped me back in. She had the tag; I wasn't even 'it' anymore. The game was my last link to the Six, now that everyone was split up. Would they forget about me?

So, when a light knock rapped across the trailer door, I felt a bit blessed. A girly knock, weak and anxious—a knock from someone who might bolt at any second. Definitely not Emily.

I rushed to the door before my dad lumbered up and scared my guest off, but found he hadn't woken anyway. From the timid nature of the knock, I secretly hoped Nora would be at my door. I smoothed my hair before opening our trailer to the world.

Cameron. Not at all who I'd expected. More strawberry than blonde, her hair curled downward in complex ringlets. She wore a long, green coat made from loose-knit wool and underneath that, a black sweater and blue jeans. Every inch of flesh covered.

Easy to see how beautiful she was, despite the clothes. Full lips, freckles, natural blush to her skin. More life than the rest of us; honeyed milk. Somehow smiling even when she wasn't. Cameron was the one who flowered.

"I need you to take this knife out of my hand," she said, staring directly ahead, eyes unfocused.

A few inches of blade jutted from between her thumb and index finger, pointing toward me. Cameron had a knife.

"What the hell?" I asked, stepping back.

"I can't give this up," Cameron whispered.

"Do you have to point it at me?" I lowered my voice, glancing back at my snoring dad.

The dagger tipped toward the ground. "I got tagged."

"What are you talking about? Just drop the knife. I'll pick the damn thing up." Didn't want to go near her.

"I'm having a rough day, and I need help," Cameron said, thick lips wrapping around each word. "I'm going to tell you a story, and then I'm going to give you this knife. Are you okay with that?"

"Of course," I said without hesitation. "Of course I'll help you. Come in. Just put that thing away, would you?"

"I can't. I have to give it to you. But first, I need to tell you why. Quick. My timer started a few minutes ago."

I didn't want to turn my back to her, so I tried to seem calm as I walked backward into the center of the trailer and motioned her into my room, extending my arms like a gentleman.

"Take my bed, please." It was the only surface in the tiny room suitable for sitting. I perched on a table in the corner, far away from the knife as possible.

"You really can't set that down, just for a minute? You're making me jumpy," I complained.

"I really can't. Let me talk. What happened to me when I was a kid, with Mr. Gimble—it changed me. Something happened to my head—not physically, but inside me. I got this knife when I was twelve. I stole it from my mom, about a month after Mr. Gimble got tired of her and they decided I would pay the rent." She rested the dagger across her palm, stainless steel blade glinting in the light. A cheap knife, one that folded back so it would fit in a pocket, with a wood-grain handle and bronze clasps. Brown rust—blood?—stained the grip.

"This thing was in my pocket for years, I took it with me every time I went to go see him. Always told myself I'd cut him open. Never did, though. Only person I've ever cut with this thing is myself." Cameron pulled the sleeve up her arm. Angry red lines, running vertical, some still scabbed with blood. At least a dozen marks, from wrist to elbow, exposing her to the world.

"I couldn't even testify against him in court. I'm so weak, Jacob."

I stood up. "You're not weak, Cameron—the fact you're alive means you're not weak. You're just hurting. But, cutting isn't helping anything."

"The hate is eating me." She opened her hand and stared into it. From a distance, it was hard to see the damage, the cuts were so light. But the edges around her palm lines protruded slightly, puffy scar tissue. "I lengthened my life lines," she joked, extending her palm.

I was somewhere between vomiting and crying. She looked at me, must've seen my expression, then sighed. "I'm weak, Jacob. I couldn't testify. Emily found me tonight. We got to talking. She told me about you two—gross, by the way—and tagged me. I wondered, you know? After no one played all summer, I wasn't sure if Eureka was gonna disappear, or what.

"But when I got tagged, none of that mattered. I *had* to choose something. The knife was in my pocket, and I wanted to give this up. I know it's wrong. I want to let the hate go. I came to you because I needed someone to see me do it. After all this, I couldn't just...throw the thing away, you know? It's been with me through a lot." Her voice began to drift at the end of the speech, as though she only now realized these things for herself. I watched her resolve waver.

"Please," I said. "Hand me the knife. Handle first, if you don't mind." I held out my hand.

Cameron stared at the cutting tool, bottom lip firmly clasped between teeth. "I don't know," she said. "Maybe talking to you was enough. This knife is one of the only things I have left of my mom, you know? As long as I don't cut." Her eyes drifted to the exit.

"What? Come on, Cameron. Don't be this way. You *just told me* about the knife. I can't pretend I didn't hear."

"I have to go," she said, standing. "This was stupid. You can't understand." Crimson hair shielded eyes; she stood and started to leave, forcing me to act.

I leapt across the tiny space, gripping her from behind, my fingers around her elbow, away from the blade. Cameron tensed, resisting me, twisting and pushing a scarred hand at my face. I didn't want to let go of her knife hand, I reached around with my other and—

—sharp pain, intense pressure and a dull ache in the center of my palm. As I yanked back, the sharp metal tip clung to my flesh; hungry, demon thing. In a flash of anger, I spun my childhood friend to face me and seized the blade with my slashed hand. I squeezed and pulled; Cameron gasped and let go, offering no resistance. I flung the dagger behind me—it clattered to the ground in the corner—and clutched my hand to my chest.

"Christ, Jacob!" Cameron gasped, tears already falling.

"It's okay, it's only a few cuts. Be strong. You got tagged, you have to do this. Do you want to disappoint me? Disappoint David?" I squeezed my blue shirt, now black with blood.

She turned soft with concern. "Let me see." Her hands gripped my arm; they were rough with scars. I winced and let her open my fingers. One deep puncture and two long cuts marred it, bleeding softly. I yanked a dirty towel from the floor. "I'll be fine." I sat down on my bed; the sight of my blood made me light-headed.

I followed her eyes to the corner of my room, where the knife fell. "Hey. Over here. Forget about it, okay?"

Cameron shook her head, then turned to me, brow wrinkled. "That's a lot harder than I thought it would be. I'm sorry, okay? I'm so sorry. But, thank you. I knew I could count on you; you're always there for us. Hell, you saved me from Mr. Gimble in the first place, and you've never asked for anything. So, thank you."

Guilt sizzled, foul chemical reaction in my chest. She'd already stabbed me; may as well bare my secrets. "I didn't call the police on your dad," I said. "Steven did."

She actually smiled—just barely, corners of her mouth flailing under the weight of her depression. "Steven told me, like four times. You think he wouldn't use that to try and make me like him? Of course he did."

"Oh. So then why'd you thank me?"

Cameron smirked. "You gave him the idea. You tagged him, you dared him to do it. It really was you, Jacob, and you never tried to take credit for it. At least, not the good parts."

Was it me all along? Did I cause Kent, Steven and Cameron to lose their homes, did I save Cameron from further abuse?

I didn't know what to think. I knew my hand hurt, though. "I am going to destroy that knife," I told her. "So I want you to put it out of your mind. No more revenge. You don't have to kill Mr. Gimble, you don't need to punish yourself. The best thing you can do is be happy. I don't know what I can say to make things any better—probably nothing, but—"

Her scarred hands clutched each other, looking lost without the knife. "There's nothing you can say. This is good, though. There's nothing fair about what happened, but I made a decision to at least change this one thing. I can stop this *stupid emo shit*."

"Cutting *is* stupid emo shit, Cameron. Play Eureka. Move past that. Plus, we're too poor to be emo. I can't afford the hair product."

Cameron smiled, at last. I smiled too; she had that contagious effect. She leaned forward, shifting her weight across the bed and landing on top of me. Arms circled me, clutching at my back; she buried her face into my shirt. I held my bleeding hand away from her, squeezing the towel as hard as I could.

"Thank you, Jacob. Thank you for being here. Thank you for being normal. Thank you for being one stable thing in this goddamn nightmare."

21. Memento mori

THE NEXT DAY—a Saturday—Cameron called our trailer's land line.

"I want to tag Steven," she said. "But I need your help to smooth things over. The last time I talked to him, things didn't go so well."

"What happened?"

"Me. He...wants to be my boyfriend. I don't see him that way. But he starts talking about how he's really the one who saved me from Mr. Gimble, and not you, like he's gonna convince me I owe him. It's stupid. But, I still want him to play Eureka. I need you to break the ice."

We discussed details for a few more minutes. When she hung up, I was excited about the plan. Steven said he quit, but I had faith he'd come around and decide to play. His decision was based off a jealousy of David, not any sort of real logic. I needed to make sure he understood that.

Things seemed simple, and were, up until Cameron arrived at my trailer with a friend in tow.

"Hi," I stammered. "Nice to see you."

Emily barked a short laugh: "Don't make this weird, please."

So it was going to be that way—the affection was gone. I downplayed my disappointment: "Why would I?" I shrugged. "There's nothing to be weird about." Except, y'know, having sex with my childhood friend and then being ignored.

Emily rolled her eyes. I decided not to give her any more ammunition, and kept my mouth shut.

I parked the car a block away from Steven's house; the girls waited while I walked up. Sure, it was a single wide, and the lawn needed mowing, but it was a *house*. Dropping out of school must've been working for him.

Pushed on the doorbell–nothing. After I rapped my knuckles across his door, it swung open.

Steven had changed. His straw hair was now molded by copious amounts of gel into short spikes, bleached at their tips. The big coke bottle glasses were replaced with small, rectangular frames, and a stud pierced his right ear.

He spread his arms; I hugged him, thumping his back with my palm. "Good to see you," I said. The words were true.

"Good to see you, too. Come in!"

The place reeked of cigarette smoke; ashtrays littered every surface. Bare walls were punctuated by a single round clock; everything was utilitarian and tidy, save the stream of smoke rising from an ashtray near his computer. A lamp in the corner provided all the light, so our shadows splayed out in gross dimensions on the walls.

He sat on a stool next to his kitchen counter.

"So, got any video games?" I asked, grinning.

"Like you wouldn't believe. Looks like you won't be holding a controller anytime soon, though. What happened?"

I held out my hand, wrapped in white bandages from the night before. "Cooking accident," I lied. "You'd beat me the same, with or without."

"Well, sit down, at least." He pointed to a stool near the counter.

I stood still. "How've you been?"

"I'm all right. Dropping out of school was the right thing to do; now I'm working, making money, you know. Life."

I didn't, but I nodded anyway.

"Hope High sucks," I said noncommittally. "Really boring."

We stood for a moment; I found myself more nervous than I'd expected. How did I broach the subject? Seconds ticked by.

"So, what's the deal?" he asked. "I get the feeling you didn't come here to catch up." Steven reached for a pack of cigarettes on the kitchen counter and lit one.

"I wanted to talk to you about Eureka." I finally took his offer, and sat down on a cheap futon. The aluminum ribs of the seat dug through the thin padding.

"Wait—are you 'it?'" Steven looked ready to run.

I spread my hands, palms facing up. "Why do you care? You quit. But no, I'm not 'it.' I promise."

He studied me behind his new glasses. "I believe you. You could never lie to me, anyway—I see right through you. C'mon, before you start in on this whole Eureka thing, let me show you something." I followed him into a small bedroom hot with electronic equipment. The sound of fans; the glow of LEDs. Spare cables hung from hooks in the ceiling. Computers were stacked side by side, some atop others, and three monitors faced him.

"Is this where you command your robot army?" I joked.

"I've been doing this data retrieval," he said, "where people screw up their computers with viruses or mistakes or whatever, and I piece the information back together for them."

"Sounds interesting," I lied.

Steven sat down at his computer chair, all mousy, folded over with nervous excitement. He turned the three monitors on. Every few moments he reached to an ashtray and flicked his cigarette.

I noticed some black ink scrawled on the side of the smoke. "What's that?" I asked. "On your cigarette."

Steven pulled the cig from his mouth and presented the tightly-rolled cylinder of tobacco between two fingers. "Sometimes I write on them. Nontoxic ink. I feel like, if I put something really important on a piece of paper and smoke it, it's inside me. Kinda stupid, I know. This one says 'who they say you are.'"

"Short for 'you are who they say you are?' What David wrote on the baseball concession stand?"

Steven glanced down. "Didn't say I never listened to him, just that I had some issues with management. Shut up and look at this."

He clicked through some files until a girl's picture filled the screen. She was about our age; pretty brunette, cherry-red lips, ponytail, cheerleading outfit.

"Is she a client?" I asked. "Good work, man. She's hot."

Steven nodded. He opened another folder, this one filled with pictures. He flicked through a few—the girl with friends, playing tennis, riding a horse. Family moments.

Another folder held her favorite music. Another, the profiles she'd built on different websites, and still another held a repository of forum posts and chat files. We spent a while scrolling through this stuff—the girl describing her first experience at a concert, her first kiss, her worst enemy, all the usual bullshit. She was honest and sincere; seemed like a nice person.

"You have her phone number?" I asked, half joking. "Seriously, how did you end up with her computer?"

"Her name is Rachel," Steven answered. "Her parents sent the computer to me."

"Why?" I asked.

"Rachel died a month ago. Car accident. They want me to put together a DVD of the photos on here. I finished it two weeks ago."

Stunned silence. I rocked awkwardly back and forth on my feet, hands in pockets, standing over Steven's shoulder. "Oh," I said. "Sorry."

"It's all right. I never knew her when she was alive. Except now, I might know her better than anyone. This is what I've been working on. It helped me get over Cameron, really."

"Get over Cameron?"

He nodded, face sullen. "She never wanted to be more than friends, you know? Kent humiliated me every step of the way, always bullying me, picking on me. Showing her my...lack of manliness. Why would she like me?" His voice tightened; he exhaled slowly, calming himself. "It's okay. There are other girls out there, you know?"

"Living girls. Living girls, Steven—this isn't an improvement. Though, y'know, I'm sure she was great. Was."

"She's beautiful," my friend admitted, skin so pale in the monitor's light that he seemed all blank, unrendered polygons. "I don't know. Could you just let this go? The computer is like life support. She's dead, sure, but I'm just now getting to know her. So she's not *totally* dead, right?"

He clicked through picture after picture of Rachel running, practicing cheers, posing with friends, eating lunch. Her image reflected off his glasses, as though projected from his mind.

"She's totally dead, man. What's the point? Yeah, she seems great, but how much does that matter, now?"

Steven clenched his jaw as he let out a frustrated moan. "I know this seems crazy, all right? I'm not an idiot. I don't know. I've been obsessing, a little. I feel like she's mine, somehow."

"Now that's just creepy, Steven. Don't fall in love with a ghost."

My pale friend stood from his chair, sighing as he did so. "I know; you're right. I've known for a while, but I figured you were here to tag me. And if that's the case, then I want to give Rachel up. I wanted to make sure you knew what you were doing, before this all started. What it will cost me."

"I didn't lie; I'm not 'it.' Listen: a living, breathing Cameron told me that she wanted you back in the game. She asked me to come here and talk to you, because she knows we're friends. At least you have a chance with Cameron, right? Better than this."

Steven seemed to brighten at the mention of Cameron. He even smiled. "She said that? She wants me to play?" He looked back at his computer. "But, you pretty much have to choose between Eureka or a normal life, right? It's a big commitment. If I play, I'm going to play all the way. Once I start, there's not going to be any stopping me. Graduation was nothing."

I smiled. "It doesn't have to be that extreme, right? You can just use Eureka to better yourself."

"That's watered-down medicine, though. Eureka works because it makes you uncomfortable. If you start filtering out the stuff you don't want to do, you'll break the whole game. Besides, if David can do it, why can't I?" Steven asked.

"Fair enough, then. The girls are actually waiting out front. You ready to meet them?"

Steven nodded, then took a deep breath. "Cameron's out there, right?"

"Cameron and Emily."

He nodded again, walking to a mirror on his bedroom wall and running fingers through his hair. A few spikes were rearranged, glasses cleaned. "Let's go."

I followed him to the front door; he pulled it open to reveal Cameron and Emily, standing side by side, grinning. "Hi," they said.

Cameron was all pink lips, tan skin, red freckles. Blood at the surface, sex and summer. Emily was monochromatic in comparison, ash and coal. She stood behind Cameron, hands in the back pockets of her jeans, looking bored.

Steven smiled back. "Just get it over with." He held out an arm.

Cameron put her hand on his. "Tag," she said, all smiles.

Steven turned back into the living room, heading for his bedroom. My stomach sank. The inevitable.

Goodbye, Rachel.

By the time I got there, he clutched the computer to his chest with one arm and yanked cables from the back with the other, unplugging the life support for Rachel's ghost. Emily and Cameron piled in behind me, watching with silent interest.

Once he'd detached the cords, he cradled the PC under one arm, staring into it as though some great truth might be revealed. Then he reached a hand into the exposed rear panel and pulled out a hard drive.

Little metal rectangle, about the size of his hand—Rachel's broken soul. Damaged digital creature, repeating the same messages endlessly and receiving none, masterless glimpse into her past.

He turned to Cameron. "Take this," he said. "Destroy it, keep it, I don't care. I want you to have it, and I never want you to give it back to me."

Cameron nodded, taking the hard drive from him. I only stood numbly, watching this exchange unfold. Now, all the light in the room came from the 'No Signal Attached' text blinking on the monitor in carnival shades of pink, blue, yellow, and green.

I heard sad choirs in my mind. Nothing left of Rachel in the world. He cherished what he'd shown me, and now it was gone. *Eureka.*

Steven gave a look that I'll never forget: equal parts desperation and determination. Nothing left to do but leave my friend to mourn. I motioned to the girls, bringing them out the door and to the car.

22. Immaculate misconception

Now

"WELL?" I ASK HIM. "Is Eureka a terrible idea, or what?"
"Maybe," Mr. Aschen answers. "There must have been a better solution than getting rid of all his work."

"Sure, he could have quietly quit, but you're missing the point. If Steven planned to be soft, to go easy, then he never would carry through. Eureka adds pressure; *we* add pressure. People aren't very good at changing themselves, but they can be if they work together. Steven's answer wasn't the best possible solution—the *best* solution takes more than fifteen minutes. But, this is the solution that'll actually get done."

Mr. Aschen only nods, expression indecipherable.

"It happened to me, too—when I got tagged," I say.

———

Senior year, December

I stretched out my hand, fingers spread.

Five points, five lines, five minutes until school ended for the entire Christmas break. My palm blocked out the teacher in front of me, who looked hung over again.

I wasn't as worried about being left out of Eureka, not with the developments between Cameron and Steven. The game working its way back into our lives was like the pressure change before a coming storm. I'd stopped smoking weed every day. Wanted to be clear and focused for whatever came; wanted to remember every second. Eureka was a jealous addiction, and wouldn't allow for any others.

"I'm bored. I've seen this episode like a billion times," Geoff moaned beside me, referring to the day's events. "Is this what man was born for? To sit in desks all day and accomplish nothing? We're achievers, my friend."

"What has mankind ever achieved?" I leaned over and whispered to Geoff.

"Uh...okay, I'll play. Airplanes? Trains, cars, the moon landing? The Internet? Pornography?"

"I think those are all complications, not advancements. What do you think life is like in the Third World?"

"A lot more death," Geoff replied.

"A short meaningful life, or a long useless one? Which is better?" I asked. "I think that's the problem with America, you know? We have everything handed to us. We don't know what to do but grab as much as we can and keep it to ourselves."

Geoff spied a female student ahead of him. "I wouldn't mind grabbing some for myself, anyway. God knows, I could use it."

"You don't, though. You don't *need* it, I mean. You just think you do."

The bell rang, and we walked together to the parking lot.

"You sure are full of advice today," Geoff noted.

"I've been noticing things lately, is all."

Someone was leaning up against my car. Couldn't tell who, from this distance. Geoff kept talking; I ignored him and tried to work out the details. Was that a dress?

"Are you listening?" he asked. "I'm dropping knowledge, here. This is how the world works."

"What?" I asked, squinting, searching for a face.

"Once a month, the fire department gets together and picks one fireman to sneak around the city starting fires. You know? They elect the best fireman. You win, you set the fires now. They should, anyway. Makes sense," Geoff said.

"Hilarious," I murmured. It was Emily. She leaned against the blue aluminum of my car, smoking a cigarette.

"I should be king," he commented. "Shit like that will take us to the top."

"I have to go."

"Because of the hot girl on your car?" Geoff asked, pointing at her.

"Yeah."

"You're my ride. I can't get a ride home because of that girl? What kind of friend are you?"

"Eureka," I mumbled. She dropped the cigarette onto the ground and rubbed it with the toe of a treacherously high-heeled shoe, then stepped toward us. "I'm his sister, Moira," Emily lied. "And you are?"

"I'm Geoff," he said. "Fan-freaking-tastic to meet you. Jacob never mentioned a sister."

"Figures," Emily said. "He's so shy about his personal life."

"What are you doing here?" I asked.

"Our vacation, stupid," Emily said, grinning behind giant sunglasses. Praying mantis.

"Right," I said quietly. "Vacation. I remember now."

I had no idea what Emily planned, but I couldn't refuse. Not after the last time she kidnapped me.

"Where are you two going?" Geoff asked, sliding over to Emily.

"I'm about to find out," I told him. "Family only, buddy. Moira, let's go."

"What the hell?" I asked once we'd pulled away from the school parking lot. "He's going to think we're actually related, you know. Jesus, Emily, what's wrong with you?"

Secretly, I was thrilled. Couldn't let Emily know that, though.

"We *are* related, at least for the foreseeable future. And you're not going to call me 'Emily,' either."

"All right. Lay it on me, then—what's the story?"

"Eureka happened. For now, I'm Moira, and I'm twenty-five. See?" Emily reached into a large black and white polka-dotted purse and pulled out a driver's license. The girl in the picture was named Moira Blocker and looked vaguely like Emily, save Moira's sunken eyes, long nose, and eight years of additional aging. Behind the sunglasses, they might pass for each other. "I'm your sister. I'm vacationing from England, where I moved when I was ten to study ballet—that's why I don't have an accent, you see. You and your dad grew up in the trailer because all your money went to funding my dance classes. I was a star all over Europe, at least until I broke my ankle on the biggest day of my biggest competition, ending my future as an international dance sensation. Now I'm bitter and lost, so I came back to my roots to find myself."

"So me and Dad grew up poor for you, and you still let us down? Even in your fantasies, you're screwing up my life. Where'd you get the ID?"

"I found it," Emily grinned, nodding toward the polka-dot purse.

"You found it," I repeated, deadpan.

She grinned. "In that purse, which I most certainly stole."

"You're ridiculous."

"It was a spur-of-the-moment kind of thing. Well, spur of the fifteen minutes, anyway. And if we play Eureka, we can't *have* anything, right? So what's the problem with borrowing what you need? I'm going to give it back eventually, whenever I'm done with Moira."

"And then you'll carefully return the ID and..." I stopped talking and sighed instead, not really caring about the purse, only wanting to argue with Emily. "Where are we going?"

"North," she said. "We'll work out the rest when we get to 'north.'"

"Where will we stay? What will we eat?"

"We'll have to make do," my temptress replied. "We'll forage. We'll be survivalists, Jacob—urban survivalists." Alabaster skin framed thick red lips I couldn't help but imagine wrapped around me. Like our first time together was designed to give her an unholy power over every other interaction we had.

I shrugged. "My dad's going to kill me for disappearing like this."

"Then don't go home," Emily said. "Ever."

I looked into the rearview mirror; Kingwood faded fast on the horizon.

"You've been missing David's lectures—he gave me this idea. Well, not in so many words, but he inspired it," she said.

"What do you mean? Lectures?"

"You should see it; we come out to his trailer, some nights. He gets a couple shots of liquor into him and just starts preaching, basically. Good stuff."

"How could no one tell me you've been hanging out at David's? I want to go."

"Well, where have you been?" Emily picked at a nail as she spoke.

"Locked away in some shitty warehouse for lazy kids. What do you think?"

"David says," she said, "there is no such thing as 'home.' He says that concept is no good for us, and we have to come to see wherever we are at any given moment as being home." His words, her mouth. Reminded me of all the other ways David got to have Emily.

"What does that even mean?" I asked.

"It's pretty simple."

That meant I couldn't question it. The conversation ended; I focused on driving, on Texas as twilight overtook us. I focused on the flat, arid landscape as it slowly grew hillier—each slope rising over the next, as we grew closer to the source of whatever geological disaster made central Texas into hill country.

I leaned back, resting one hand on the wheel. "I miss you sometimes," I said.

As the words left my mouth, I braced myself for impact: I knew she'd have some clever quip, some way of telling me to be a man. Some way of comparing me to David.

"I missed you, too," she said.

As night began to wrap around our little metal box, I pulled into a small, sleazy motel in a town somewhere in North Texas. I'd been further north before, with Dad, but I'd been a kid then and didn't remember my way around the state. Emily had fallen asleep and was stretched out over the passenger seat, legs splayed lewdly on the dash, leaving me to drive in silence.

I'd dreamed of running away, of exploring the world, of course. And here was Emily with me, my partner in crime. Liberating—but there was this bit of despair tugging at my chest, too. Was I homesick already?

Emily stirred as I pulled to a stop. "Where are we?"

"I think we're in Rusk, wherever that is. Population 1,021, the sign said."

"So, why are we stopped?"

"It's late. I'm hungry and tired. We're at a motel."

"I could drive." Emily yawned, mouth pulled wide. She stretched, breasts jutting skyward, such perfect circles you might use their curve to do your geometry homework. "I'm all rested up, now."

I imagined Emily drove like she lived.

"No thanks. I think we should both get some rest. Besides, where do you want to drive *to?* We have no idea where we are now, right?"

"True," Emily said. "I guess we're far enough away. All right. Let's get a room."

"How?" A question of logistics—I'd never paid for a motel room, and I didn't have any money.

"You are such a kid," she answered in disgust, reaching into Moira's purse and applying fresh makeup, lips smacked together to smear the crimson clay around the delicate curves of her mouth.

I followed her swaying hips out of the car and into the motel office, where a tired looking old man leaned back in an office chair and watched a small television.

He ignored us. Emily tapped a bell, which clanked uselessly, then cleared her throat. "We need a room." The little impostor seemed cool, like she'd done this dozens of times. A deft hand slipped a small green wallet out of the purse, flipping it open. She handed him a credit card and Moira's license.

I was hit with that same wave of fear, just like breaking into the school's office. *What if we get caught? Will this guy turn us in?*

"I'm her brother," I said shakily, as though that explained something. The clerk stared at me for a moment as Emily leaned backward on my foot with her heel. I winced and shut up.

He spent a long time looking at the ID, then back at Emily's face. She stood with her chin tilted slightly upward, as though daring this man to question her.

"When's your birthday?" the clerk asked.

My voice caught in my throat. He was onto us. We were screwed. I'd have to call my dad from jail.

"July 6, 1986," she said without hesitation.

The man shrugged, apparently satisfied. He ran the card then handed the plastic rectangle back to Emily.

"Room 26," he said, handing her a key. The older man sighed and leaned back into his chair, refocusing on the television.

"What the hell?" I asked Emily as we walked through the cool night to our room.

"What? That went pretty well, I think."

"You're stealing."

"Wait a minute, Mr. Holier-than-thou. Don't *you* do drugs?" She slid the room key into the door. A green light pinged.

I stopped. That was buying weed from a friend at school for twenty bucks, not snatching a purse and using the credit cards. This seemed different, more dangerous somehow. "Aren't you worried we'll get caught?"

She pushed open the door, reached in and turned on the light. "No. Where do you think I got these clothes? No one ever gets caught for this stuff."

I doubted that, but didn't argue. The door to the room opened. The little chamber was three times the size of my room at home. Hard, stained carpet and a noisy air conditioning unit next to the window. Looked like luxury, to me.

Emily jumped onto the bed, staring up at the ceiling, stretching her arms and legs across the mattress. The strap of her dress drooped from her left shoulder, revealing a black bra. She sighed contentedly.

I wanted on the bed with her. As I approached, a palpable force pushed back. Nervous tension so real it made me weak. Still, I pushed through, into her personal space.

I sat on the sheets, far away as possible, perched on the edge. Felt like I was introducing myself to an animal at the zoo, stepping into the cage.

She leaned up and stared at me, bottom lip between her teeth.

This was it. Which Emily was I getting? Would this trip be romantic, or not?

There's a ten second pause; I know because I'm counting every breath. "What are you doing?" she asks.

"I thought, y'know. There's only one bed. Plus, we're on this adventure together, and..."

"You want to have sex again," she said flatly.

Do I? She used me last time.

I liked it, though.

True. "Yes."

Emily turned, dress hiked up around her thighs, and leaned across the mattress. Her hand extended, slowly, slender fingers pointing toward my shoulder.

Yes.

She pushed me. I fell two feet off the side of the bed, landing with a thud on my side.

No.

Giggling erupted from the bed.

Red-faced, I settled with taking the cushions off two chairs and using them as a makeshift mattress on the floor, which wasn't much less comfortable than my bed in the trailer.

Too embarrassed to talk. I turned the TV on instead. We watched it together; me on the floor at the foot of the bed and her sprawled out across it, until at last Emily decided she was tired. I closed my eyes and listened to the rhythmic creaking of the ceiling fan over my head.

Just as I drifted into unconsciousness, Emily spoke: "Oh, and by the way. I talked to your principal. They're willing to let you back into KHS. 'Night, Jacob."

Blink, blink. Miles from sleep. Toss, turn, repeat.

23. Diva

BY NINE, when Emily groaned her way awake, I'd probably gotten an hour of sleep.

I could go back to KHS. Nora was there, and I'd have the chance to see her again. Then again, here I was with Emily, riding the wind, doing something I'd daydreamed about. Exploring.

Yet in every practical way, Emily—as a person, at least—was a bad choice. Except, she was so damn exciting. Washed the boring right away.

"You've gotta be starving," I intoned, staring up at the ceiling from my spot on the floor.

"I'm a little hungry, yeah," Emily said, "but I need a shower more." She yawned and stretched her arms out, black dress mangled from the night's sleep.

"There's a Dairy Queen across the street. I can go get us something while you're getting cleaned up," I said. "I don't think you want me here while you shower anyway, right?"

"Why? You're not a peeping Tom, are you?" she asked, grinning.

I stared blankly ahead. Any answer would set me up for a sucker punch. If I said I wanted to see her naked, she'd disappear. Opposite answer, and she'd tease me until I did, then disappear.

She stood and stared for a few seconds, chewing a fingernail. "All right, all right. Do whatever you want. Get me something with eggs in it."

As I turned to leave the room, I got one more look at her. Emily admired her own reflection, running fingers gently through her hair. She began lifting the dress from her body just as the door slammed behind me.

The morning air was lukewarm; the surface of my car was covered in tiny beads of dew. I reached into my pocket and retrieved the keys I'd been sleeping on all night, pulling them out of their place embedded in my thigh.

The car door opened at the same moment the door to our room did. Emily stepped out, wrapped in nothing but a towel.

I froze with my hand on the keys and the keys in the door. She spoke before I worked up the willpower to look away from the looseness of the towel on her breasts. "Don't you need some money?"

I sighed. "Yeah. My bad."

Emily looked at me sideways for a moment then shrugged, handing me a five-dollar bill with her free hand. She turned and walked back into the motel room, bare feet padding across cracked asphalt of the parking lot.

I sat down in my car. *Shit.* Almost out of gas; the needle was a centimeter from the big orange E.

I drove across the street to the nearest drive-through and got Emily something with eggs in it. As I returned to the room, she was dressed again and looking refreshed.

I, on the contrary, was exhausted, and my head hurt. "So, where to today?" I asked her.

"North," she said. "North, until we find some reason to go east. When we do, we'll go east."

We made our way back to the car, taking our places. I sighed and put it into gear, pushing off into the stream of the small, two-lane highway. Within moments, we were out of Rusk and back into the hilly wilderness that made up central Texas.

We drove north for about five minutes before I decided to bring up the obvious. "We're going to run out of gas. We need to stop and fill up."

"Next station you see," Emily said.

A few moments, then I couldn't hold back any longer: "Why did you talk to my principal? Why did you get me back into KHS?" I asked her.

She dug through the purse on her lap. "I called, pretending to be your aunt. I plead your case; the principal was okay with it. I think he forgot all about you, really."

"Yeah, but why?" I asked.

"Same reason as always. You need to have options when you choose me. Everyone does—you can't arrive here inevitably. That's meaningless to me; I don't want to be common sense, or the best thing you have going right now. You choose, or it's not a choice."

More Emily madness. I slowed and turned into a gas station, cringing as the underbelly of the car bottomed out on a steep bit of concrete. We pulled up to a pump.

"So, what do you think?" she asked.

"About what?"

"About Kingwood."

I hesitated. I wasn't sure, to tell the truth. Nora sat in the corner of my mind, beckoning me, not allowing herself to be forgotten. I knew she was disappointed I got expelled, mad that I didn't take better care of myself. But if I could prove myself to her again, I thought I could probably get close to her.

"I love the freedom," I offered.

"You're about to tell me something I don't want to hear," Emily said, leaning back and crossing her arms.

"I don't know," I answered. "I don't know if I'm ready to leave for good."

I stepped out and took Moira's credit card from her. Pump was too slow; I stared back and forth from the meter to the tank.

After a moment, she followed me out of the car, circled around and got close. Eyes locked on mine, couldn't see anything else.

What did she have planned? Heart raced. I knew she was no good for me, I knew it was unfair—but when she was close, it didn't matter.

Our feet fit together like teeth on a zipper.

"You really do care about me, don't you, Jacob?" Emily asked, staring up at me, eyes wide.

It happened again; everything went away and there was just the intensity of her presence. "I do, but..."

"But, what?" Emily sighed. "Why does it have to be complicated? We're on an adventure. Roll with it, Jacob. I'm ready to really do this. I'm in, Eureka is what I want from life. Let's stop dicking around, there's a world out here. Look at it. You can't try to control things and play this game at the same time. Let's run away! We'll watch out for each other, we'll teach other people how to play."

"I can't. I feel like I left things at home. Loose ends." I avoided mentioning Nora. "I have too much going on to leave and never come back. Not yet."

Emily clucked her tongue, breaking eye contact, staring down at the cement. "I can't do this with you if you don't really want it. Not because you think you'll have sex with me, or because you're scared to disappoint me. That's worse than being alone."

I started to object, but couldn't. "I care about you. A lot," I said. "But, David—Cameron, Steven." Just left with the nouns; everything else melted through the sieve.

The gas pump clicked. The tank was full. "Prove it, then."

Emily kissed me without warning, lips pressed hard to mine. Briefly, though, then she pulled back. "Tag," she said.

The ground dropped below me, my stomach bottoming out somewhere around my ankles.

She watched me expectantly. Any given moment, and everything could change. I looked out at the gentle hills around me, farmland dotted with a few houses. Green squares cut into the earth. Not even big enough to be a town, but still—this was her trump. I blame the death of David Bloom on the profound beauty of Eureka.

Whatever I was debating about going home or staying with Emily would have to wait. I had to drop it all, right then, and change my frame of reference. Never a dull moment.

I reached into my pocket and retrieved the car keys. One hand wrapped around Emily's neck; I pulled her close, kissed her cheek once then put the keys in her hand. "I'll see you someday," I said.

Emerald eyes wide. She twirled the keys on an extended finger before clutching them in a pale hand. "You'll see me again," Emily said, hips swaying as she opened the car door and climbed inside. "Good luck out here."

I smiled; the door to my car swung closed. The vehicle shifted into gear and Emily drove off, leaving me stranded.

24. Awakening

Now

"I HAD TO DO IT," I explain. "I signed up for this experiment—eagerly, too. I think it will enrich my time here. What Eureka does to you comes in two parts. The first part is changing your identity. Everyone gets put into a stereotype, something that can be packaged and easily understood. Guy with glasses is a nerd, muscular guy is a jock. Mr. Aschen, you look like an old college professor, and you're a counselor. That's your part. I grew up in a trailer park, and that's mine. Shakespeare said life is a play, and I agree—the issue is, the casting sucks.

"But, Eureka makes you unpredictable. Helps you get away from those stereotypes holding you back. And when you are forced to act outside of your assigned role, you start to understand what bullshit the whole system of having roles is." I lean back in my chair and stare at Mr. Aschen.

He looks up from his notepad. "What's the second part of Eureka?"

"The second part actually changes you, the player. I loved the car while it was mine—but, not too much. The car was temporary, one way or another. Even if it didn't get stolen or wrecked, I'd get tagged and have to let it go. So, I loved the car, but it didn't tear me up to give it away. That's how everything is. Everything you have, anything you own that you try to take pleasure from, is going to go away eventually. Better not to rely on material stuff. Eureka makes sure you don't."

Mr. Aschen is gray and drying; his skin is drawn tight over tall cheekbones. He cannot properly twirl the pen, but he can shuffle it back and forth between gnarled hands, and does so constantly.

"Other than David, what do you think made you want to play Eureka in the first place?"

I study my socks so he can't see me smiling. "It's like we never had a fair chance. We grew up in this shithole, our parents failed at life, and even if we tried as hard as we could, made all the right decisions, worked two jobs and saved up money—we could never have half of what was given for free to everyone around us. So, the life in store for us was already a shitty deal. Even if I did everything right, my life was still going to be second-rate, at best."

"But if you were building things..." Mr. Aschen raises his hands helplessly. "Careers, contacts, college—that's how you escape the trailer park. How can you throw away every opportunity you get, and then be upset at life for not working out the way you want?"

"I *don't* want it!" I lean forward; my voice rises. "I don't want a manager position at Wal-Mart. I don't want to be an accountant or a paralegal. I want...I don't know what I want, but I don't want any of that. There's no option available to me that would make me happy, so I choose none of the above. Look at you, Mr. Aschen. Is your life perfect? Everything going flawlessly? What has your life of hard work gotten you? I'm willing to bet your life is still shaped by a series of coincidences over which you have no control. Eureka is my way of accepting the way life is. Accepting, and rejoicing."

My psychologist leans back and folds his arms.

Goddamnit, Emily.

Trapped in a wide open space.

Plenty of options, sure. Just, they all began with a hundred mile walk. The gas station behind me had a pay phone, but I didn't know anyone to call and had no money to call them with.

Embrace the change, Jacob. Could be worse.

Right. Positive attitude.

I started walking, following a small road running perpendicular to the highway, back behind the gas station. Trees, birds, flowers.

Nice day, cool winter breeze. This was it—a real adventure. Completely alone.

Lots of walking. After about a half hour, I came across a shaded camping ground filled with RVs and picnic tables.

An old man rolled hotdogs across the rusted iron grate of a community grill; three men stood at his side, supervising with beers in hand. Their respective old ladies sat in lawn chairs, reading magazines. A geriatric looked up at me and smiled. Caught me off guard—I smiled back.

A large Christmas tree stood in the center of the camp. Totally forgot about the holiday; gift giving was not a big deal in my family. Not being at home saved me the awkwardness, really. I didn't want more stuff.

Did kind of miss Dad.

I didn't want to go into the RV camp and disrupt what looked like a private party—but I didn't want to keep walking, either. I found a tree twenty feet away from the nearest camper, sat down and leaned against it.

Hundreds of miles away, and still in a trailer park. But, this wasn't like Broadway. These were expensive RVs, ten-wheelers with big windows, the kind you didn't hook up to a car.

After about an hour of sitting underneath the tree and rubbing my temples, I was approached. One of the older ladies—maybe watching a distressed youth in the Christmas season was too much for her.

"Hey, sweetie—would you like a hot dog?" All cautious care, like the puppy might be rabid.

"Um," I mumbled, "Sure. I'd love one."

She extended a plate with a fully assembled hot dog. I smiled, thanked her and quickly ate the food. As I chewed, I realized what I must look like, sitting there in my dirty clothes, staring woefully at the group of wealthy, elderly folks.

Well, this was survival. I figured if I was going to do this—going to play Eureka, and be willing to wander, then I needed to learn how to survive. Begging was not out of the question.

"Thank you," I told her. "That was great."

"Are you from around here?" she asked, painted lips smiling gently. Gray hair curled, red blush too thick on cheeks. The grandmother I never had.

"I'm just hitchhiking through," I lied. "Looking for a place to sleep."

She clucked her tongue, moaning pitifully. "You poor thing. There's a bathroom over here, with showers too. Why don't you come and eat some more? We just keep cooking and cooking, with no one to feed."

Shocked, how nice she was. This was new.

"I don't want to intrude," I said. "I'm just passing through. I can sleep right here, you know." I patted the ground.

"Oh, dear, I can't possibly sleep in that big RV all night, knowing you're laying out in the grass without even a blanket or a bite to eat. Come on, come get some food. I think Ron has a spare sleeping bag, I'll see if we can help you. Come on, I won't stand for you being miserable: come eat."

I'd happened on a group of retirees, traveling America, enjoying each other's company. For the most part, they seemed happy to have me around; after a couple hours of uneasiness, they began asking me questions, telling me stories. Trusting, to a certain point. No one let me inside their RV, but they were happy to talk with me and share their food. I slept near a campfire, with two pillows and a sleeping bag.

Not half bad, for my first night.

By the second day, a Vietnam veteran was familiar enough to loan me a set of oversized plaid sweats to wear while they washed my tired t-shirt and jeans. I looked like someone's lame grandson on Christmas morning.

In the evening, the camp came alive. People played guitar and sang and talked and drank. I listened to their stories and asked questions, and they seemed happy to have me. I even kind of enjoyed my time there. I hadn't got this sort of attention since... well, ever.

What's more, I still woke up Jacob Thorke. Despite having changed everything—despite the fact I wasn't in Kingwood and David, Dad, Nora, and the rest of the Six weren't around—I was still me.

Something deeper defined me, something other than relationships or cities or routines. The game worked; Eureka took me somewhere new. Made me experience something unexpected.

I was happy to spend a second night.

During the third day, I was approached by the woman who gave me the first hotdog. "We're shipping out today," she said, big silver hoops of earrings bobbing in time with her words. "It's about that time for us. We're gonna head north to the next camp, or else we won't make it to Canada by summer."

For a minute, I thought about asking to go with them. I'd been polite and well-behaved, and they seemed to enjoy my presence. Still, I couldn't. I mean, I was 'it.' Someone needed to get tagged.

So as they packed their things, I racked my brain for some way out of there, for someone who might come and save me. I needed to find a phone, but first I needed someone to call.

There was one person I used to call constantly. My fingers memorized the pattern the numbers made when they pressed across the keypad. By twitching my fingers across an imaginary phone, the digits came to me.

I didn't want to call this number. Still, this was the only one I knew.

I walked over to the woman who'd been so generous with me all week and asked to use her phone. She didn't hesitate to let me.

I dialed the ten-digit sequence.

"Hello?" the voice of an older man.

"Hi..." I said, trailing off. Didn't expect this.

"Can I help you?"

"Yeah, sorry. May I please speak with Nora?"

"One second." I heard the phone being put down as Nora's father went to fetch her. Christmas music in the background; I could practically smell the cookies.

After several excruciating moments, the phone was picked up then put to Nora's ear. The sound of her hair brushing the receiver made me smile.

"Hi, Nora. Happy holidays."

"Jacob?" she whispered. She apparently didn't want her dad to know who was calling. "I'm with my family. What are you doing?"

"I...just wanted to call. See what's up."

"Nothing is up. It's Christmas vacation," Nora repeated. "My aunts are down. What else would I be doing? What are *you* doing?"

"I'm kinda in a situation, actually."

"When are you *not* in a situation?"

I cringed. "Yeah, you're right," I admitted. "Look, I got back into the high school. I'm going to spend my last semester with you. At school, I mean."

"Well, good for you, Jacob. But I'm not going to pretend I believe you, or that you're suddenly going to stop ruining your life."

"I need you to pick me up," I blurted. "I'm in Martindale."

"Where the hell is Martindale?"

"I'm not exactly sure. It's north of Kingwood, I know that. If you drive north on Highway 71, you'll get there in a couple hours. I'm stuck here, alone, until someone comes to get me. I'll be walking down the highway, if no one gives me a ride. Where's your Christmas spirit?"

No response; only the sound of a receiver clicking down on its rest. The line went dead. I sighed and flipped the phone closed, handing it back to its owner.

"Are you sure there's nothing we can do for you?" she asked, eyes searching mine. The RVs were packed and running, ready to go.

"I'm sure," I told her. "I'll be fine." Knowing as the words left my mouth, I wasn't and wouldn't be.

"Where are you going to sleep?"

"I'll..." I gestured lamely off to my right. "I'll find some place."

"Here. Take this sleeping bag, so at least you'll have something to keep you warm."

I hesitated.

"No, just take it. I cannot, in good conscience, let you stay out here like I know you are going to, without this. You sure you don't want to use the phone again?" she asked.

I assured her I'd be fine, then waved goodbye to my surrogate family as one by one, the RV group lumbered away from Martindale, migrating like geese in search of year-round moderate weather.

As the last RV left the clearing, I sighed. Alone again.

I spent a few hours walking around the campground in circles, trying to formulate a plan. I could wait for the next RV to come, and hope they'd be equally generous, or I could start walking south toward Kingwood and hope something happened along the road.

Ultimately, I decided on the road. So, with the sleeping bag under one arm, I began walking back home.

I kept my thumb out as I climbed hill after hill, measuring the passage of time by each crest I conquered. Breaking down the journey into these tiny increments seemed like progress, though even as the sun peaked over my head and fell to the right, I knew I'd only gone a few miles.

Late in the afternoon, the first car stopped for me. A woman in her late forties. When she noticed the sleeping bag, though, she pulled away without hearing anything I tried to say.

I felt torn between tossing the sleeping bag so I'd seem more like a stranded motorist, or running the risk of having to spend the night with nowhere to sleep but a cold ditch.

Before I made that difficult decision, though, an old white Thunderbird screeched to a halt at the crest of a hill.

I stopped and blinked a few times. The car maneuvered an angry U-turn and skidded into the southbound lane, finally coming to a stop near my feet. Smelled like burning rubber.

The window rolled down and I peered inside.

"Just get in," Nora said. I opened the door and climbed in before she changed her mind.

I couldn't stop smiling. Nora was clearly angry, though; tanned hands gripped the steering wheel, knuckles white. Her jaw pulsed in her cheek from the strain she put on it, and those cocoa colored eyes were curled into cruel half moons. Hadn't seen Nora in seven months. She'd lost a little weight. Thought I even saw a little blush on her cheeks.

"I hate you so much," she said, voice deadpan.

"Do you?" I asked. "Look, never mind, don't answer that. I'm just glad you came and got me. I was literally sleeping outside, on the ground, with no money and no one to call. *On Christmas.*"

A rumbling growl expelled from Nora's throat; a deep sound I didn't imagine could come from her. A sound like all the angry stuff she wanted to say was boiling inside. "And now I'm spending my holiday picking you up, Jacob. And do you know why? Because I'm an idiot. Because I like you, and I hate it when you're in trouble. But really, if I was the smart, proud person I know I am—then I wouldn't be here, would I? So I must not be very smart, or I must hate myself. One or the other. Because I'm positive, the reason you were stuck out here is *that stupid game.* Am I right? Tell me I'm wrong. Please, tell me I'm wrong, Jacob."

"You're right," I said, looking anywhere but at her. "It's the game, but it's not—"

Nora shook her head. "Shut up, Jacob. I don't want to hear it. I don't want to sit here and try to talk you out of throwing away your future. I'm just going to be an idiot and enable you and let you get back to doing it—but at least don't make me hear your justifications the whole way back."

Silence ensued. Honoring her request was the least I could do.

I studied Nora's face as she drove. Eyes moist, lips pressed tightly together. With the way she was acting, maybe she did care about me.

Better not to test her. Instead, we sat in awkward silence the entire drive back. As we grew closer to Broadway, I knew soon, the adventure would be over. I'd be back at the trailer, back to my dad and school, and back to the Six.

I was 'it;' at least I had that going for me.

Nora braked hard on the road outside the trailer park. I opened the door and turned to face her.

"I hate you," she repeated, staring forward.

I think she meant the exact opposite, but I didn't tell her that. I only smiled, thanked her, and shut my door. Her tires kicked up gravel as she slammed on the gas, putting as much distance between us as possible.

I sighed and stared at my trailer. Almost sad to be home, back to my life as a normal kid who lived in Broadway and went to school in Kingwood. Before, I'd been a drifter, and I was capable of anything.

Grackles beat their wings, rising away from the tall oak across from me, a brown-black eruption of mad synchronicity. Their squawks welcomed me home.

I stopped outside the door to the trailer, realizing I'd have to explain to Dad where I'd been for the past week, and what happened to the car. I wondered what I'd tell him.

Could say lots of things. Could have been an extended field trip, or maybe a kidnapping. Wasn't far from the truth. But when I walked in, his back was turned to me and he had a cup of clear liquid in his hand, vodka bottle beside the chair.

All my wild imaginings were for nothing, because he supplied the answer for me: "I see you're out of jail," he grumbled.

"Yeah, Dad," I said sarcastically. "I'm a free man. By the way, your car got stolen."

My father jumped up from the couch and swayed on his feet. "What?"

"I went to Rusk to see a girl; I met her at a hotel. When I woke up, the car and the girl were gone," I lied. My father's face turned blood red and I sensed a tremendous outburst pressurizing inside of him.

So I left. Rather than sticking around, I got out of the trailer and roamed the dark for a few hours until he passed out. Might have been better off if I'd never come home.

25. Aftermath

Now

THE DOOR OPENS. We stop talking and observe the detective who fills the frame. The officer looks tired, face bloated with exhaustion, balding head covered in sweat. He twists to force himself into the tiny room and slams the door shut behind him; Mr. Aschen jolts in shock at the sudden sound.

"Do you think this is a game?" the detective asks, his crotch uncomfortably close to my face. "We don't have all day, kid. You need to understand the decisions you make now are some of the most important decisions you will ever make in your life. This isn't a counseling session. This isn't time to work out your issues with your girlfriend. There's a good chance you won't leave this jail until a jury of your peers decides your fate. We need to know what happened to David Bloom."

I meet his bloodshot eyes with my own. "I told you exactly what happened to David—someone shoved him off a water tower. What I'm telling you now is what lead him there. We've reached the beginning of the end, Detective. I am still coming to terms with what I know. Let me talk through the events with this man. You'll learn everything I know, I promise."

The police officer locks gazes with Mr. Aschen. Complex signals are sent and received through rods and cones within the eyes of each man; data is transferred through the light waves between them and something is understood. The cop shakes his head, running a hand through his thinning hair, then opens the door and walks out, slamming it again. This time, Mr. Aschen's pen flies all the way into my lap.

A nice pen, heavy. I hand the writing utensil back to him.

"Thank you. I apologize for the intrusion. Now, where were we?" he asks.

I begin again.

⸙

Senior year, January

I woke up at ten to the sound of our trailer's phone ringing. I reached for it out of reflex, hoping not to wake my father on a weekend. We'd been up fighting all night.

"Hello?" I asked.

"Jacob?"

"Yeah. Who is this?"

"It's Geoff."

"Oh. Hi, Geoff. Long time, no talk," I said, wincing. Definitely not a good time. Besides, now I knew I was going back to KHS, and talking to him felt awkward. "What's up?"

"Where you been, man?"

I paused before I blurted out: "Crazy busy. My sister—you met her, right? Well, she came in, and she's been taking up all my time. Plus, me and my dad are fighting, my car got stolen, you name it."

"Sounds ridiculous man, you'll have to tell me the story some time. I got a car, actually, a piece of shit station wagon, but it runs." He began to talk excitedly about the car.

"Geoff," I interrupted him. "I actually need to be going right now; my dad and I are in the middle of World War Three. But, call me again. I want to catch up."

"Oh, all right," he said in a way that was obviously not 'all right.' "I was hoping we could hang out...but I can see you're busy, so anyway, I'll let you get back to that."

I sighed and hung up. I heard my father's sheets shuffling in the other room and didn't want to fight anymore. I'd been trying to convince him not to call the cops on Emily—no luck.

So I got out, throwing on jeans and shoes before he had a chance to say anything. Spent my afternoon walking back and forth across Broadway and the surrounding forest, like I was twelve years old again. No escape.

I remembered Emily's comment about the Six hanging out at David's trailer in the evenings. Gotta be worth a shot; as the sun set I made my way through the woods. The trailer's path was overgrown, and it took some wandering before the sound of laughter drew me toward my friends.

I wished I'd brought a flashlight to show me the way. Instead, I stumbled over hard roots with dusk at my back and twilight before me. Stopped about ten yards from the group; a campfire outside of David's trailer lit their faces with a dancing glow. I heard the murmuring of their voices, watched them as they stopped to nod knowingly toward David. Emily was absent, which was disappointing.

Cameron sat nearest to where I stood, staring distantly into the fire. I wondered if her wounds were healing, or if she'd found another way to hurt herself.

Kent hovered near her. Forehead and jaw all met at strong angles, thick arms and wide shoulders, fat dripping from the muscles like upholstery hanging from the ceiling of an old car. An entirely different kind of monster than the hunched over, glasses-clad teen to his right.

Steven perched on a tree stump, nesting over fresh white sneakers. His knees were drawn up to his chest and wiry, pale arms rested atop them, chin on top of those. Every few moments, he pushed his glasses back up his nose. Gaunt frame was folded up like an origami figure of himself, like viewing him from a different angle might render the boy invisible.

All attention focused on David. He paced back and forth and waved his hands as he spoke, shadows cast from the fire painting his face in stark contrast. A half-full bottle of whiskey sat near his chair.

I cleared my throat as I walked the last few dozen feet to the fire.

He stopped talking and turned to face me. "Jacob," he said, voice vaulting through the trees. "Great of you to join us. Welcome back to the fold."

"Nice to be here," I said lamely. I hadn't seen all these people together in a few months; felt like showing up to a birthday party without an invitation.

The others mumbled their greetings.

Eager to be out of the spotlight, I filled a gap in the ring across from David. The moist feel of Kingwood forest on my ankles; I ran my palm over a patch of clover. Some things never changed. "What have I been missing?"

"We're just talking," Kent said. "David was telling us about liminal spaces."

"Liminal?"

"Liminal spaces are places between places," Steven answered smugly. When he was positive about a bit of knowledge, he showed it off like that—he'd been making the same satisfied grin since he was five years old.

"What does that mean, exactly?" I asked.

"I...I mean, David was explaining," he finished. I looked across the circle to Mr. Bloom, the only one standing. The modest trailer served as a backdrop, and his shadow loomed there.

"A liminal space is a transitional period. Imagine taking a train ride from Kingwood to Houston—where are you while you're on the trip over? You're not in Kingwood or Houston, you're in the liminal space between. With Eureka, you never get off the train. The doors slide open, you look out and notice, then start moving again." Orange fire cast him in amber hues. "Every stop won't be a good stop. Sometimes you are going to suffer. But that's life, condensed. Play Eureka, and you'll do more living in a decade than most people could do in a century. "

A log split over the flames and a shower of sparks rose, a swarm of fireflies climbing into the canopy of leaves above us. "Who is 'it?'" David asked.

I answered: "I am."

"Tell us your story. Who tagged you, what happened?" he asked.

I stood, staring into the measured fury of the smoldering fuel as I spoke. "Emily came for me while I was leaving school one day. She had this idea to just drive north, so we did. We spent the night in a motel, but we had an argument the second day. She tagged me, and I gave her my car. I guess she's still out there somewhere, driving around. I spent a couple of nights at this camp ground, and then hitchhiked back here."

Wide-eyed praise. Steven clapped his hands together. "Well, shit. You gave away your *car?*"

I shrugged. "It's only a car. I wouldn't want to sit around and miss it all day." Even though I kind of did—but they didn't need to know.

"I do believe that sets a new standard," Steven exclaimed, firelight dancing across the thin, rectangular glasses.

"It's not," I said, feeling awkward at the adoration. "It's not nearly as impressive as what David did at graduation."

"I disagree," Steven said, big smile on his face. "I think it's better."

What are you doing? I wished Steven would shut up. He looked a bit too pleased with himself.

"Well, it was certainly something," David said, stiff-backed, both hands on his head, shadow warped into monstrous dimensions on the trailer behind him. "I'm proud when all of you finish tags. When Jacob does something great, it's just like if I did. I'm that close to you guys."

"Then what about Kent? He hasn't done anything." Steven again, pushing buttons.

"Well, no one has tagged him lately. Jacob, why don't you do the honors?" David asked.

I glanced over at Kent. "Isn't that a lot of pressure to put on the guy?" I asked. Really didn't want to walk over there; wasn't sure if he still hated me or not.

"I'm sure he'll be fine, Jacob. What's making you so nervous? Are you scared of Kent?"

Kent stood, reminding me how much bigger he was. "Stop talking like I'm not here. And, why would he be scared of me? Just because he put my dad in prison and ruined my life?"

I looked at Steven and opened my mouth. He shook his head.

I stammered: "I didn't..."

Steven spoke: "I bet he'd just try to kiss Cameron again."

Goddamnit. He was pushing everyone's buttons, playing us against each other. The crimson in Kent's ears looked purple in the flickering lights.

"Hey, c'mon, you can't make me tag someone," I protested. "I mean, I get to choose. Kent should go like normal, this is, this..." There was no way to phrase it without making things sound worse.

David's face hardened. "Fine. If you've got to be a pain in the ass about it, and make it all dramatic, then don't tag anyone. I'll just go."

My response sputtered and died on my lips.

I sat down back at my seat, as far away from Kent as possible. David walked over to the fire and retrieved a burning branch, waving it like a conductor's wand as he spoke. "We'll start with the root of the problem: homes. People are too attached to them. A home will always be your enemy. If you start to get connected to one area, or you set roots down in one spot, it'll be harder to escape when someone tags you. Your home becomes a shrine to your identity, too, telling you every day who you are. It's hard to be anything but my mother's son when every moment I'm in this home reminds me of her."

David faced his mom's trailer, burning branch in hand.

"If, on the other hand, you set yourself free from this—and along with it, set yourself free from your friends, your family, everyone—then you become free yourself. You don't let your possessions own you. The entire world is your home.

"Because, trust me," he continued, "you will change, your situation will change, and your home will change. There is no solid ground, and there is no answer. Take fire, for instance. A house fire is the closest your average person will ever come to playing Eureka, if they're lucky enough. Fire cleanses all the baggage that made you who you were. It keeps you from staying stagnant in a shifting world. Change is the only constant; we need to embrace change." He lowered the burning branch underneath his trailer, so the chemical reaction licked at the plastic.

Flames began to spread as the acrid smell of melting plastic filled the air. David kept moving and repeated the process all around his home, each time spreading the fire further.

Finally, the luminance burst up into the trailer itself, and the door was sucked against its own flimsy frame as oxygen was consumed with the inferno. David smashed a window with his elbow to revive the conflagration with a fresh breath, and the blaze shot up even higher. At last, he tossed the branch inside and stepped away.

I blame the death of David Bloom on the fact that after the math, David always won. We sat back in awe. He spun, and we were trapped in orbit.

26. Mouth or mouthful

Now

"DO YOU KNOW what a narcissist is, Jacob? I mean, the clinical definition?"

"Someone who's really conceited, right?"

Mr. Aschen leans back and folds his hands, gnarled knuckles protruding. "Sort of. As a clinical term, it refers to someone who is incapable of realizing other people are as valid as himself. He never minded frightening other people, or forcing them into dangerous situations, or even damaging their property—because he never could understand that they didn't deserve to be hurt. To David, other people were just robots, or worse, insects. Lesser beings."

The counselor continues: "But a side effect of narcissism is not being able to process social interactions. How can you deal with other people, if you don't think they're really people? How can Mr. Bloom feel guilty for burning down houses, when the people he hurts don't matter? You might as well feel guilty for kicking over an anthill. But he was still human, and when David needed to process those feelings, he relied on scapegoats. If a failure came from David, it was the fault of someone around him. Someone else set him up with an impossible task, or let him down at a crucial moment. Every person in David's life was there for a purpose, a tool to be used. To boost his ego, or to take the fall. It all needed to fit into David's illusion that he was an incredibly important and valuable person."

"I was supposed to be his conscience," I say. "He told me that, when I visited him after graduation."

Mr. Aschen snorts out a laugh. "Narcissists don't have that level of foresight, Jacob. If they did, they wouldn't be narcissists. He was using you, remember? Trying to actively balance himself would mean he recognized his condition, which would negate his being a narcissist in the first place."

"David was aware of the way his mind worked. He may have been full of himself, I'll give you that—but he kept other people in mind, too. I'm the one who let us down."

Mr. Aschen leans forward, arms on knees and hands crossed, forcing me to lean back. Can taste the cheap coffee on his breath. Want out of this room.

"That's nonsense, Jacob. You're proving my point right now."

"I was supposed to be his conscience, and I was starting to have doubts. I didn't let him know, though. I failed him," I say.

***

Senior year

That night, we sat and watched David's trailer burn in effigy to our collective childhoods. No words; nothing to say. All of us had something in our past we wanted to wipe clean, to purify in fire. Some, more than others.

Kent sulked at the edge of the clearing, unwilling to rejoin the group. Cameron stood with him, murmuring into his ear occasionally, rubbing his shoulder. The inferno subsided as the trailer was reduced to smoldering plastic, melting into some pitiful mutant thing, hissing and popping. The fumes got to be too much for me; I got up, dreading my return trip. Less than a mile to the trailer park, but I'd have to stumble through the woods again.

As I walked past, Cameron spoke: "Wait." I turned and looked; a white light flashed in her palm. "Want to walk with us? You'll eat less spider webs." Kent stood behind her, big body acting as a frame in which she stood.

I'd love to walk with Cameron—not so sure about Kent. I'd avoided him for the past year, ever since I took the blame for calling the cops on his dad. We'd never resolved the conflict, and I never wanted to.

"Sure," I said. The word didn't come out like I wanted; no strength behind it.

We walked with Cameron between us, drifting toward the road, chasing the flashlight's beam as we diverged around trees and thorny bushes.

Neither Kent nor I could speak; the tension was too thick. Cameron cut through it: "Are you okay not getting tagged tonight, Kent?"

He shook his head: "I...it's embarrassing." The towering teen's voice resounded at an octave lower than mine. "Why do I even have to beg in the first place?"

"Maybe everyone is just looking out for you, in their own way," Cameron noted. "Maybe your head isn't in the right place to be playing Eureka."

"But that's what you want me to do!" Kent exclaimed in frustration. I got the feeling this was a long-standing argument between them. "I just want you to be proud of me." Kent lowered his voice when Cameron tugged at the black sleeve of his howling-wolves shirt.

"I am proud of you, Kent," Cameron said. "You're like a big brother to me."

I cleared my throat, annoyed at being forced into their private conversation.

"I don't want to be a brother," Kent whispered, as though I might not hear it despite standing right next to him. "Can't we talk about this alone?"

"Sure," I offered. "I'll stand right here until the sun comes up—don't mind me."

Cameron spoke: "Don't be stupid. You can walk with us; we aren't going to leave you out here." Cameron waggled the flashlight back and forth to demonstrate where 'out here' was. "Kent, we talked about this. You know I like David."

This was news to me. "David?" The name flew from my mouth before I could stop it.

"Well, he doesn't believe in relationships yet, but yeah. We've been talking about it. Nothing official, so far." Cameron stated matter-of-factly.

Who wasn't David sleeping with?

"Well if he doesn't believe in relationships, you can't ever really get together, can you?" Kent asked helplessly.

"So I should just give up?" she asked. "A lot can happen in the future. We're always changing, after all."

Kent pulled Cameron and the light away from me, behind a tree. I stood in the absolute dark, starlight blocked by the canopy of leaves above. The flashlight outlined the space between their bodies in a pale glow, a tight parenthetical. Their whispers came clear through the night, despite his efforts.

"I'm not giving up, either. Wouldn't going to prom with me be a big change?" Kent asked. She hesitated, didn't respond. "I swear, Cameron, if you give me one chance, one night, then you would change your mind. I know it."

Painful.

"Maybe," Cameron sighed. "I don't want to talk about this again." The flashlight appeared again, leading the way. A moment later, we broke through the woods and arrived at the road. We stopped at her car.

She sat down in the old red sedan and turned the key; headlights broke the night. Cameron handed me her flashlight. "Night, guys."

Kent walked to his truck, which was parked nearby.

I walked up to Kent. "Hey, man, I'm sorry about all that. No hard feelings, okay? It may not seem like it, but I didn't tag you for your own good." I extended a hand. Mainly, I wanted a ride back.

Kent's fist flew forward, below mine, and hit me in the stomach. I doubled over as the air evacuated my lungs, struggling to breath.

He got in his truck and shut the door. After a moment, I caught my breath and stood. I sighed and flipped on the flashlight. It flickered for a moment, then died. I shook it, feeling the batteries rattle inside until the light flared up again.

I made my return to Kingwood High School a week later. Not much to it; no one seemed to notice I ever left. Starting midyear sucked, though—everyone was used to their classes, and I still needed to find mine. Didn't care too much. I only needed to last four more months, and then none of high school would ever matter again.

My first two periods passed without incident. I killed time by actually taking notes, which I'd never done before. My third period, Advanced American History, was interesting. Nora was in it—so was Cameron.

I picked a seat right next to Nora. She didn't acknowledge me.

The teacher launched into a discussion of the Battle of Chesapeake Bay. As she lectured, I listened with one ear while devoting the rest of my faculties to watching Nora out my peripheral. Deep brown eyes seemed to trap all light entering them, storing it somewhere out of reach from people like me. Dark pools.

Brunette hair curled at the tips of her shoulders, a little bit of makeup. Not glamorous by any means. More like glamour's younger sister, who was never let out of the house because glamour herself slutted it up at first break. Everything subtle and downplayed, blue jeans and a cotton jacket, soft and smart and accessible.

At the end of the period, the teacher passed around a short quiz about her lecture. Since the class had almost ended, the hum of low talking filled the room, which the teacher made no attempt to quell.

I made it through most of the quiz without issue, but was stumped by a question about where the Lucitania sank. I turned to Nora. "Hey, could you give me a hint about this one, or tell me where to look, maybe? Please?" I asked, trying to sound calm as sudden nervous electricity nearly shocked the pen out of my hand. Needed to see how she'd react.

Nora turned to look at me, and I knew I'd made a mistake. Bitter. "I believe it happened in the water. You know, where the drowning is." She ripped out her answers to the quiz, slammed her notebook closed, and crammed her things into a backpack.

Stupid. I cursed myself and guessed the other answers, turning in the quiz just before the bell rang.

I rushed into the hallway and caught Nora. "Hey, sorry about that. I should have known the answer."

She ignored me.

"But hey, thank you so much for coming to get me over the break. It saved—" I didn't have time to say 'Christmas' because a shove sent me flying into the lockers so hard my feet left the ground. Nora chuckled, but didn't miss a beat and kept walking.

I staggered to keep my balance. When I turned, I saw Kent walking the other way.

27. Chased

KINGWOOD HIGH WAS A BUSY PLACE, so I didn't run into Kent every day. Half of the time he was out for baseball, and I managed to avoid him some days.

But, when Kent did corner me, the torment was relentless. What's worse, some of his teammates idly joined in the hate—because high school students, it seemed, loved finding reasons to be angry.

In between Pre-Cal and Speech, Kent slapped the books out of my hands, sending them sliding across the hallway. While everyone laughed, another athletic-looking kid kicked my math book like a hockey puck over the floor, where a group of them began a makeshift game with it.

Some enterprising minion of Kent's filled my lock with Super Glue, so I walked around the school with a backpack weighed down by seven enormous books. I'm Jacob Thorke, and I'll be your sherpa today.

Some parts of the baseball team started working to one up each other, seeing who could trip me in the halls, who could dream up the worst insult. I was used to that sort of shit, but this was a new kind of hate. I'd always been picked on, but passively—because of what I looked like, where I was from, and not some sort of personal vendetta against me. Kent was pissed.

I happened across him as he dug through his locker after school. Despite his large frame, he didn't look like a grown man. Rather, he was still the same chubby kid I always knew, just warped out of proportion. Literally a gigantic second grader, instead of the fully formed adult I expected.

"Don't you wish you could do this?" Kent asked.

"What, rummage?"

"Open your locker."

I shrugged. "I keep 'em all on me. Simplifies things."

"Yeah, and it makes you look like a fag," he accused.

"Do homosexuals have big backpacks? I wasn't aware. Besides, I don't care what other people think of me, Kent. Maybe if you played Eureka, you'd know that."

Kent slammed his locker shut. "If you would have tagged me, sure. You could have given me a chance with Cameron, but you'd rather embarrass me, make everyone think I'm an idiot. Then you say it's my fault you don't tag me, that it's for my own good. That's the problem with you, Jacob. You always think you know what's best. You don't know shit."

Kent turned to face me. The heat from his anger radiated off his face. He flexed his shoulder, and I leaned back. He took deep breaths and seemed to be undergoing some mental exercise. After a few moments, he moved back.

"It's like when you called the cops. Smart, right? Save the whole park, be a hero. You know what happened after all that? Foster care. Yeah, great. You think that was better for Cameron than her home? Dad already stopped molestin' her, that hadn't happened in years. You brought it all back up, ruined our lives, for nothing. Because you thought it would help."

"I just did what was right," I said. About time I took responsibility for it.

"What was right." Kent glanced back at the abandoned hall then leaned in uncomfortably close, face inches from mine. "You know what happened thanks to all your fucking rightness? Dad was out of jail in three weeks. Came back twice as mad. Took it out on me every day for months. Yeah, what's right. You think you're so goddamn smart, all you do is make things worse. That's the worst kind of stupid, thinking you're smart when you're not."

"Wait, what? Three weeks?"

He snorted out a laugh. "No evidence against him except that phone call you made. Cameron wouldn't step foot in court, and I don't blame her. He got in some trouble for the way he ran the park, that's it." Kent turned away from me, swallowing hard, grinding teeth evident from the taut skin of his jaw. "All I can do now, is keep her safe. You know what it's like to know my Dad did those things to her? I'll spend the rest of my life trying to make it up. I have to."

"I'm sorry, Kent. But you and Cameron isn't going to happen, and she's glad I called the cops. She told me."

"Oh, great. Jacob Thorke is sorry. If you woulda kept your mouth shut in the first place—"

Poor confused bastard. "Your dad's the one who screwed this up! Don't blame me."

Kent's face contorted, eyes widened. His fist balled up again, rising into the air.

I flinched impulsively, shutting my eyes. When I opened them, Kent had turned and was walking away.

But, that look in his eyes. I knew it, had known it all my life. The grackle killer.

Nora hadn't offered to kill me in nearly two weeks, so I thought my odds at successfully having a conversation with her were as good as ever. I ran to catch her after school, which wasn't easy with my gigantic backpack.

"Nora," I called. "Hey."

She turned. Zero reaction on her face, but at least she stopped. When I reached her, she started walking again. Just our footsteps echoing down empty halls.

"Would you like to not go to prom with me?" I asked.

"I don't want to go to prom with you," she said immediately, voice flat. "I hate everything about prom. And you."

"You didn't hear me. I'm asking if you'd like to *not* go to prom with me. Together. We'll go somewhere else instead, on prom night. Screw prom."

Nora cracked a smile. Triumph. Trumpet fanfare; love and light.

"I knew you were in there," I said.

"Jacob," Nora said, "I've been thinking about this a lot, and I'm not mad anymore. It's as much my fault as yours. I care about you— I do. But, you don't care about yourself. And you want me to have to worry about what happens to you? That's just cruel. Until you start giving a damn about your own future, you can't ask me to do the same."

She continued: "I will maybe not go to prom with you. I need time to think about it. Carry these books for me."

Suddenly, things weren't so bad. This was more than I hoped for. I took her books from her.

"I want you to know," I said, "I think you're beautiful. The reason I never asked you out is because you always made it sound like it was impossible, like being my girlfriend was some insane idea." We stopped at the exit doors and turned to face each other.

Nora turned and smiled at me, caught herself, and forced a serious look back onto her face. "You really are a good guy, Jacob. Something has you convinced you're not. If you actually decided to try at life, you might find you don't suck at it." Eyes met mine.

"You're not seeing the big picture. Life is more than good grades or a paycheck." Eureka. We both knew it, even if I didn't say it.

Nora took her books out of my arms. I wanted to clutch at them, to draw them back to me. She only shook her head, opened the door and stepped through.

About halfway down the first road to Broadway, I heard the obnoxious buzz of an unmuffled pickup truck, followed by an intimidating horn, bleating like a cow in labor. As it grew closer and more urgent, I got a strong hit of dread. I knew, somehow, that the sound was coming for me.

Three of them, in Kent's red truck. It angled straight toward me; I stepped out of the way, and it roared by with only inches to spare. Hot exhaust and the smell of burnt oil followed. Baseball practice must have let out.

I heard shouted insults in Doppler Effect as the truck passed. The moment it crossed me, Kent braked, leaving thick black tread on the pavement. He climbed out of the driver's seat and two of his friends unloaded from the passenger side.

All I needed to see. I abandoned the backpack and tore off, running with the road, hoping to get away. Their shouts and laughs were dulled to a menacing growl in the back of my head.

A body crashed into mine; I was tackled to the ground. I kicked and punched at Kent's face, managing to free myself from his grip around my legs. I scrambled up, pain cascading across my back. Without turning to face him, I darted across the street; my entire consciousness centered on the dull, rhythmic thud of my feet. No one else in sight.

Couldn't outrun him. Kent gripped me by the shoulder and swung me off balance, sending me sliding over the asphalt. My palms skinned against the small pebbles like cheddar over a grater. The other two were jogging up. They looked worried, maybe in over their heads.

We were interrupted by a high-pitched whine—the sound of an engine pushing itself to meltdown level. Kent stood, stepping aside and leaving me lying flat in the street. I rose, turning to see the incoming car. A blue flash skidded out of control, sliding sideways, stopping perpendicular to the road as my attackers scattered to avoid being struck. I lay dead center in its path, staring at the approaching door. It stopped feet from my body, rocking on its tortured suspension.

Not just any car: it was *my* car.

"Come on! In you go," Emily said, kicking the door open for me.

Didn't need to be told twice. I leapt in and slammed the door shut, hitting the lock a split second before Kent tried the handle. I strapped my seatbelt on as Emily peeled away, tires spinning for a moment as Kent kicked uselessly at the bumper.

"What are you doing here?" I asked, turning around in my seat and watching Kent and his friends run back to their truck, sparking it to life.

"Would you rather I let you out?" Emily asked, taking her foot off the gas.

"No!" I shouted. "Go. Just go! They're following us."

"Why?"

"Because Kent thinks I ruined his life. Or he wants me to tag him. Or he wants to impress his baseball friends; I can't tell. He's crazier than you are."

Emily grinned. "Nope." Her hair was cut short, and she sported electric pink lipstick that made her look more than a little like a stripper—which, no telling, she might be.

"I want to hear all about whatever the hell you've been doing," I told Emily as the truck gained on our subcompact car, "if we don't die today."

A traffic light; cars idled at either end of the split road. The green arrow for a protected left turn lit up. She veered into that lane without slowing. Emily pulled the parking brake up, skidding into the turn at forty miles an hour. She couldn't make the angle; it was too tight. We flew over the grassy median, into oncoming traffic, narrowly avoiding cars lined up at the red light by aiming behind them.

Someone didn't get out of the way in time; we clipped their side mirror, sending it flying in a shower of black plastic and glass. Emily didn't stop, forcing her way upstream in the lane, then turning into the driveway of a gas station. Hitting the curb at full speed sent me flying; the seatbelt snapped around my shoulders, throwing me back down. We blasted through the station and onto a side street. She turned onto this and kept driving, albeit slower.

"He's gone," I said, checking behind us. Thought I might black out from the rush of adrenaline and panic. "Please stop. I think I'd rather get caught."

"Someone was chasing us?" Emily asked, smiling wide. She turned onto a quiet residential street. A few more blocks and she squealed to a stop, once again deploying the parking brake and fishtailing into the shoulder of the road, smashing my face against the glass.

The moment the car stopped, I opened the door, unbuckled my seatbelt and practically fell out. I sat on the curb, head between my knees. Skidding uncontrollably into oncoming traffic had that effect on me.

Emily stepped out and stood over me, holding her arms open in a mock hug. "I'm back!"

"Hi," I groaned, staring up at her face, head framed by the fading sun. "Thanks for saving me. Please, never do that again. Oh, and my dad reported the car stolen. Don't get caught."

"Me, or Moira?" she said, smiling, before getting back into the car. The front tires spun, kicking loose rocks onto my clothes. Just as abruptly as she'd appeared, Emily was gone.

28. All fires, one fire

TIME TO DO SOMETHING about Kent.

I didn't want to—not exactly. I pitied him, honestly. No matter how big he was, he didn't have the strength to handle the truth. I wasn't the reason his dad was an abusive asshole, and Eureka wasn't the reason Cameron didn't love him. Right now, though, it looked like he wasn't going to understand that on his own. Fighting back was the only way to get his attention.

I laid low until lunch, and managed to avoid being harassed too much between classes by staying within eyesight of teachers and principals. Not exactly *fun*, but survival rarely is.

When lunch came, I snuck away from my usual "find a chair and be ignored" ritual and found Cameron and Kent. Kent was surrounded by the baseball team; stacks of muscle and fat cracking the same jokes to each other endlessly, laughing and guffawing, food in oily globs flying from wet lips.

I wasn't a fan.

Cameron sat next to him, looking lost, surrounded by skin.

Tried to look natural as I approached the table, but they spotted me coming. Two of them stood immediately, brows furrowed, shoulders hunched. Dogs barking at passing cars. Still—needed to make this quick.

I came up behind Cameron and put a hand on her shoulder. Kent turned, dangerously close, but let this occur.

"You win, Kent," I said, staring him in the eyes as I did so. "Tag."

And then I walked away to watch. Cameron stood, knit jacket and blue jeans, every inch of skin covered, as always. Kent stood as well; the rest of the table watched in interest. Cameron turned to walk away, but he cut her off, lowering himself to one knee in front of her. His head still reached her shoulders.

She tried to step around again, but he grabbed her hand. "Cameron, would you go to prom with me? Please?" he asked, eyes moist and wide, staring up at her. Some sick parody; broken white knight and the princess of scars.

Cameron pushed his hand off hers.

We watched as she crossed the cafeteria to the nearest fire alarm and pulled it, yanking her hand away as purple dye spat from its red mouth.

We all met eyes for one, two, three seconds and *briiiiiiiiiiiiiing.* Flashing lights and sirens.

A gentle tide of students began moving toward the exit, in no hurry to end the fire drill. Kent stood, watching, jaw slack.

Cameron, Kent and I stood still as the cafeteria emptied; rocks on the beach as students streamed around us. What failures we'd wrought.

By the time school let out, I was actually *happy*. Now Cameron was 'it,' and Kent wouldn't have a reason to bug me. I knew he'd be angry at first—that there'd be some retribution—but the war was almost over. Kent didn't have anything to fight for.

I spotted Nora carrying a bundle of books home, and waddled up to her with my massive backpack. "May I?" I asked, arms extended.

"Knock yourself out," she said, smiling.

My smile grew a smile; I was that happy.

Then we turned a corner. Kent was waiting, close-set eyes and little stubby nose all red and puffy from crying.

He didn't look at me or say a word as we walked past. So, of course, I couldn't resist. "Have a good day, Kent," I said, double-smile beaming through my voice.

"Fuck off," he said, banging his head against a nearby locker.

"Don't say that," Nora objected.

I stared at her, as surprised as Kent.

She continued: "*You* fuck off, and leave Jacob alone. He never did anything to you."

"Would you shut this bitch up?" Kent said, turning to face me now.

"Don't talk to her like that," I said reflexively, surprised by the power in my voice.

Good as it sounded, though, my legs froze as Kent approached. My center of gravity seemed to fall around my ankles. I saw the hand moving toward me in slow motion. As it connected, Kent's fist filled my entire view. I fell backward and banged my head against the linoleum floor with so much force, I blacked out for a few seconds.

Nora let out a little yelp and ran.

Kent stood over me, rubbing a red fist. "I really hate you. You didn't have to do that."

I tried to say something, but was too shocked by the taste of blood in my mouth.

Both of us were interrupted by Nora arriving with the principal in tow.

I got treated by the school nurse for my injuries, including an icepack on my swollen lip that hurt more than helped, and a cheek full of gauze. In the meantime, Nora flitted between the principal, to whom she told everything, and me.

She was a star student, the cameras backed up her story, and no one knew anything about Eureka. Kent would get the same punishment I'd gotten. He'd finish out the year at Hope High, now officially a *bad kid*.

I thought I'd feel better, but was still pretty shocked by the whole thing. I'd been prepared for a punch from Kent for weeks, figuring I'd move, or block it, or something. Of course, he was meaner, stronger, and heavier than me, so all that was fantasy.

Didn't help much that as I left the school an hour and a half later, I saw Kent wearing handcuffs, being escorted to a police cruiser by two officers.

I turned to Nora, trying to voice a question through the gauze that still filled my cheek. "*Mmff?!*"

"They found drugs in his locker," she said. "Pot. It serves him right."

I remembered when they'd unceremoniously cut the lock off my locker and dumped the books into a box to be shipped to Hope High. But weed and Kent? It didn't mix.

I contained my reaction. Would only make Nora suspicious; I knew she hated the game. Instead, I shrugged.

"Thanks for standing up for me," she said, smiling.

I raised my hands and nodded, which could have meant anything, but hopefully meant "It was nothing" to her.

As I stepped into her car, I saw an old white luxury sedan across the school parking lot. A thin, pale young man with spiked blond hair and thin rectangular glasses stood, leaning over the hood and watching us. Smiling.

Steven had no business being at the high school. Made me wonder.

That night, I couldn't sleep. Instead, I sat in my tiny cell in the trailer and ran my tongue over the cut in my lip. Couldn't get the day out of my mind. Seemed like there could only be one person responsible for Kent's arrest.

Kent shouldn't have gone to jail. That was too much.

Did Steven mastermind it? Seemed extreme. Made me a little bit afraid of my nerdy friend—if he could even be called that anymore. But, he'd gone to extreme measures to protect Cameron before, and this might fit his definition of 'protection.'

I was shocked out of my stupor by a fierce knock on the door—the kind of aggressive, unrelenting knock that cops use. I hurried through the trailer to where my dad snored into the face of the TV, shifting half awake at the racket. I crept past him and opened the door.

Cameron. She had a wild look in her eyes, and was drenched in sweat.

"Kent's gonna do something stupid," she blurted. "You've gotta come with me, now."

I let the trailer door slam behind me. Her car was already running, and I got in without bothering to ask any of the questions which would've been prudent, like: *Where the hell are you taking me?*

However, not asking made me seem so much cooler. "Isn't Kent in jail?" I asked.

"His dad bailed him out in an hour," Cameron answered, knuckles white from gripping the wheel, or perhaps the mention of her abuser. She sped down the road and barely twitched her neck to check the cross streets at each red light before blasting through.

"And then what?"

"They got in a fight. Knocked the crap out of each other for a little bit, then Mr. Gimble left. That's when Kent called me. I never get within a hundred yards of his shit-stain father. Anyway, Kent came to me and we talked; he is not taking this 'me and David' thing well. Or the thing with his father. Or the thing where he got kicked out of school and arrested. He needs help—I need help."

"I didn't play any part in this," I said. "I swear, I didn't. Someone else put the drugs in his locker."

"Yeah, right," she said, rolling her eyes.

"Seriously, I'm not that clever. I didn't think of any of this."

"I can almost believe that. I don't care. Look, I did something stupider."

"What'd you do?" I asked as we squealed around a corner.

"I tagged Kent. I felt bad, and it seemed like the only way to shut him up. But, he started begging again. Even after I told him we weren't going to happen. So I turned him down, again. But, Kent... he's kinda got a temper. Sometimes he loses it and keeps rolling in one direction. He doesn't stop well, not on his own."

"Yeah, I've noticed. Then what happened?"

"Emotions. A nervous breakdown? He's coming to terms with his dad, with things about David—he's trying to fix himself, to fix what happened, so that I'll like him. He said he's going to be like David." Hysteria under the surface of her voice; sea monster beneath the depths. After a few deep breaths, Cameron spoke again: "I don't like Kent, not romantically. But no matter how many times I tell him, he keeps saying Eureka makes anything possible. It's like he can't—he can't let it go."

Cameron spun the steering wheel; I banged my head against the window. She tore into a parking lot, past a rusty station wagon and a few decrepit minivans, before slamming on the brakes. Kent stood outside a second story apartment with a red plastic gas can in his hands. His left eye was bruised and swollen, almost shut.

I jumped from the car. *So this was what 'being like David' meant.*

"Don't do it!" Cameron called up to him.

"It's genius," Kent exclaimed, voice hoarse. "I can get back at Dad, erase my past, come on. What's not to like?"

Kent put the gas can on the ground then raised a white rag with one hand and a cigarette lighter with the other. He sparked the lighter and a small orange ember lit up the night. One eye wide and wild, the other bruised closed. Kent laughed, but tears rolled down his cheeks.

He lifted the flame to the rag and the infant inferno licked it nervously once, twice, and finally took its first bite from the material. The rag in his hand lit up.

There was a problem with Kent's plan to be like David, of course. There were five other apartments in the building, connected to his own.

"Come on, Kent. I'll go to prom with you! Don't start that fire," Cameron pleaded.

"Do you mean that?" Kent asked.

"Yes! Forget about the game. Just put the fire down."

"Do you forgive me?"

"There's nothing to forgive," she called back. Any chance at Kent putting the fire out was quickly dying; the orange disturbance in the air reached his hand.

"I did this for you," Kent said, lowering the burning rag.

"It's okay. Just come down from there. We'll talk," she said, curls sweat-soaked and stuck to her forehead.

Seemed like he might relent; he started to lower the rag. But, Kent's hand ignited where gasoline spilled. In another tiny explosion of orange, his shirt caught fire as well.

In a panic that only being on fire can bring, he ripped the shirt off and began flailing his glowing hand through the night air. In the process, he kicked the plastic can of gasoline, and some part of the fire's infernal consciousness saw opportunity and leapt.

There was a much larger eruption of light; the devouring elements tore into our world, climbing up Kent's doorframe and wrapping the entrance of his apartment.

Kent stumbled away from the unholy portal and into the railing, nearly tumbling over the second story walkway while batting at the flames on his pants. I watched, frozen there, as the chemical reaction reached across the curtains of Kent's apartment, then climbed up the wall. From my vantage point below, I could only see the furious amber light amplify exponentially, a gradual explosion, starving maw demanding more. The fangs of its ever-teething mouth breached the shared wall and the incandescent glow began to reflect through the neighboring apartment's window as well. Devil feast.

"Call 911!" I shouted to Cameron. I ran to the nearest door and began slamming my palm against the panel. I kept yelling, trying to warn the inhabitants of the threat. I moved to the window and pounded my fist on the glass, shouting all the time.

When Cameron reached Kent, I stopped, spellbound for a split second, and watched. Flames whipped around the two of them. She tugged at his arm, but he wouldn't budge, so she did the next best thing. Cameron slapped him—once, twice, three times, the sound blending in with the crackling of timber. "You're going to kill someone!" she shouted. "You're an idiot."

He stared at her, mouth agape. "David..." he said.

I tore my eyes away and began banging on the next door, shouting again. Someone came out: a small boy and his mother, both in tears. At the sight of the door opening, a strange feeling welled up in me, somewhere underneath the raging torrent of panic —like how even a small rock at the bottom of a river causes a disturbance. I couldn't shake the sensation I'd been here before.

I reached the third and final door on the bottom floor and banged on it. My knuckles ached, so I used my feet, too. Another set of people came staggering out.

Cameron managed to drag Kent down the stairs and away from the fire. He swayed, either drunk from the acrid fumes or weak from the depression and shock. She shouted indecipherably, punching and slapping at the boy's broad chest and face.

He didn't look her in the eye—just stared downward, occasionally reeling from a well-placed blow.

I ran up the stairs to the first apartment on the second floor and received such a shock to my memory that I stumbled and landed face-first on the steps. I recovered and skipped the apartment, going past it for the one neighboring Kent's.

I'd never been there at night before; everything looked different.

This was where Geoff lived.

I banged on his door and shouted as the heat from the fire curled the hair on my arms and threatened to consume me in its gluttony. I tried looking through the window, but the smoke was too thick. Orange light glowed from the inside of his apartment, and I prayed my Hope High compatriot wasn't home. I kicked at the door once, twice, but it didn't budge.

I hammered my fist onto the windowpane until it shattered. Reaching through, I cut myself on the searing hot glass, then burned my fingertips on the metal of the lock, finally twisting it and getting past the barrier.

Geoff's body lay on the couch, facing upward, on the opposite side of the living room.

The second my foot crossed the threshold, I pressed against a near impenetrable wall of heat. As I took another step, the air was stolen from my lungs and the strength baked out of my muscles.

I put a foot down and pulled forward, then felt the eyebrows melting from my face as searing hell ate its way through one wall of his living room. The air was sucked from my lungs—couldn't take another step, couldn't breathe. Tears welled up in my eyes; the devil evaporated those, too.

I don't remember stepping back out of the apartment. Maybe my body did it automatically, reaching for oxygen like a panicked diver swimming for air.

The breeze of the night felt unnaturally cold in comparison. I gulped in soot and smoke and dashed back inside. The shared wall between Kent and Geoff's apartments glowed, pulsating reddish orange—the wall itself turning to balefire. Layers of my skin tightened, blistered. I choked for air, lungs burning. No matter how much I wanted, I couldn't force myself further.

No hope.

At last, I turned and ran to the parking lot, jumping down the stairs four at a time. Kent sat on the hood of Cameron's car, and Cameron watched me. I felt where the fire torched the hair from my face and arms. My skin was flaky and tight, like brittle plastic wrap.

I ran straight to Kent and pulled him by the shoulders down onto the pavement. He didn't resist. I kicked him, aiming for his head but instead glancing off his ear. I tried to kick again, but a weight rushed into me, knocking me to the ground.

"Stop!" Cameron shouted, her body pressed against me, arms wrapped around my chest and arms, trapping me.

"He killed Geoff." I choked on the words.

She pulled me close, hands on my shoulders, hugging me. "The fire department will be here soon. Don't make things worse. It's okay." She did not sound like she meant it.

After a few moments, after the blinding rage seeped from me and into the cold cement, I shrugged her away and stood up.

Kent lay curled up on the ground. I walked over and pulled him up to face me. "What'd you do that for?" I asked.

"I didn't mean to," he blubbered, tears and snot running down chubby cheeks.

"You killed my friend," I said, voice calm now, like scolding a child. "Eureka isn't about getting people killed."

He reached out to my arm and gripped my torn skin in his hands. Somewhere through the snapping of timbers, he voiced the words: "Tag. Get it off me. You take it."

29. Nature/nurture

Now

"DO YOU THINK KENT COULD EVER ESCAPE WHO HE WAS?" I ask Mr. Aschen. He seems tense in his chair, leg folded and pressed against the wall. One hand clutches his folder and the other, his trusty metal pen.

The counselor sighs and looks up at me. "This is one of the big problems with modern psychology. To a certain extent, people are shaped by their upbringing, and also by their genetics. We are not sure exactly to what degree these things control a person, but—"

"Seems to me like they control a person a whole fucking lot." Telling the story is like digging my fingers between the stitches in a healing wound and ripping them out. Geoff died.

"But Eureka ultimately led to this accident occurring," Mr. Aschen protests. "David is selling snake oil—he is pretending to have the answers to your problems, telling you Eureka can change who you are, giving you false expectations."

"Why wouldn't Eureka change who you are?" I ask. "Isn't your identity just the choices you make? What could be simpler than making new choices?"

"It's not as easy as that. Not everyone can just change who they are by making a few new choices and—"

"So what exactly do you do for a living, Mr. Aschen? Don't you go around telling people how they can change their actions? If Eureka doesn't work, isn't what you do also a sham?"

I continue: "I've seen the stats, Mr. Aschen. People with abusive parents are more likely to become abusive, people with criminal parents end up going to jail. Call it genetics or the way they are raised, I don't care. Kent wanted a way to change his past. He wanted a way to rebel against what his father turned him into. What would you have told Kent? That he was doomed to be an abusive loner?"

My counselor shakes his head, clearly lost for words. I pick up the slack:

"But, for this one incident, I agree. Eureka seems responsible; or at least, Kent couldn't handle it well enough, and he made a stupid decision. Geoff shouldn't have died. It wasn't lost on me; I quit the game."

Now he looks up, alert.

———————— ✧ ————————

Senior year

The fire burned like a virus that infected the Earth, an infernal hunger destroying its host and eventually itself. By the time the firemen arrived, the top half of the apartment was in flames, and a crowd gathered around us. Kent was restrained, crying in the back of a police cruiser, face pressed to the glass. Big smudges where his tears ran tracks through the sweat and grease to collect on the car door.

Two fire engines parked at angles to the building, and great streams of water arced from the hoses down onto the structure. Where liquid met flame, steam misted into the air, glowing in the light of the fire, so the building was engulfed in a radiant haze.

About twenty minutes after the fire died down and only the blackened ends of the apartment's skeleton smoldered, Mr. Gimble arrived.

Cameron jolted at the sight of him; I gripped her arm. She pulled away, but I held firm. We watched from the opposite end of the parking lot, hidden behind parked cars.

Mr. Gimble ran from his car, screaming, toward his home. Halfway to his apartment he tripped, fat stomach reaching the ground first, springing his forehead onto the cement with force.

Paramedics assisted the landlord up and then restrained him as the obese, middle-aged man began howling in rage, cursing the medics for keeping him from surveying the damage, cursing the firemen who stomped through his home with big rubber boots, cursing God for cursing him.

This was Mr. Gimble. Forever: victim.

Cameron broke free. I reached to reclaim her, but wasn't fast enough and instead followed at a close distance, ready to pull her away if needed.

She approached Mr. Gimble as he raged against the firemen and paramedics. The adrenaline I'd thought was dead surged again; recycled acid much harsher the second time it flooded my veins.

"I want you to know," she announced to him. He looked up. At first—rage, but then something else crossed his face. Surprise. Sadness. "You made all this happen. You raised Kent in a way where this was the only thing he knew how to do. You are a blight on this Earth and no one has ever benefited from knowing you. The quicker you commit suicide, the better off the human race will be."

Confronted by the girl whose life he'd destroyed, by the mess his son made, Mr. Gimble could do nothing but stare at the ground awkwardly.

I wanted to start punching him. I wanted to get in his face until he had to admit he was shit, until he had no choice but to own up to his crimes. But Cameron needed this much more.

She stared at him, disappointed and disapproving, but not angry.

Realizing she wanted an answer, Mr. Gimble opened his mouth. "I never had..."

Cameron's eyes narrowed and he shut up. More excuses. The reason Kent and Cameron lived with such a heavy burden was frustrating, barbaric and simple: Mr. Gimble never blamed himself for anything. It was pointless to try. No good or evil in the world, no swarm of grackles to alight from the trees and attack the landlord until all that remained were clean bones.

Just excuses. Cameron turned away from him, shaking her head.

I saw myself in the side mirror of an ambulance. Scary. Almost half my hair, gone. A neat cut ran the length of my forearm and blood dripped down my wrist and into my palm, a souvenir from breaking the window.

I didn't hear anything anyone said to me; I went on autopilot again, responding with one word answers and numbly shaking my head.

By four a.m., the paramedics and police let me go home. Kent was arrested after being checked for injuries, back in jail for the second time that day, presumably for much longer.

I didn't need to ask about Geoff. I already knew the answer.

No chance at sleep. I took a pair of Dad's clippers and stood in the mirror, staring at my face. Felt ancient, looked like shit. Purple bruises under my eyes, hair burnt. Couldn't get rid of the smell.

I switched the mechanical razor into action; it vibrated against the burnt skin on my hands. I squeezed until the tingling sensation turned to pain, then dropped the guard onto its lowest setting and ran it over my head. I watched as my hair fell in clumps into the sink.

Too angry to cry—angry at Geoff for not getting out of the apartment. *Was he drinking? Was he already passed out when the fire started? How was he just lying there?*

Angry at Kent, of course, and almost as sad for him. He'd tagged me at the last moment, but who could think of completing it then? Shaving my head would have to do. I was pretty sure these extenuating circumstances would satisfy my contract with the Six; no one *died* before.

Instead of sleeping, I stared into the mirror for what must have been an hour. My father was a familiar snoring lump on his cot; an infomercial blared on the television. I didn't bother to tell him what happened.

The next day I skipped school, granting myself a three day weekend. I spent all my time alone until that Sunday, when Geoff's funeral was held. Had to call the town's two funeral homes to find out when it would be.

Nora heard what happened from someone. She called me, asking what she could do to help. I told her about the burial and she agreed to come with me. Real concern in her voice. One small victory: she dropped all pretense of playing hard to get. She'd forgiven me. I didn't dare bring up the fact Eureka was involved in the fire. I wanted to enjoy this truce before her pride convinced her to push me away again.

So we stood side-by-side in the back of an empty church, except for one older man who sat across from us and three crying women in the front. The chapel was barren and the ceremony was quick and to the point. No body to show and little to say. A preacher who'd never met Geoff read about the sting of losing someone who was so young and of all the promise he had left to fulfill, and whatever, whatever.

I hung my head and thought about when I'd ignored him. I knew he had problems, and he tried to reach out to me—me, of all people—for some sort of guidance or friendship or compassion. I'd offered nothing, because I'd been too caught up in my own little world.

Nora sat by my side for the service and the wake. I saw what I assumed was Geoff's mom or aunt or grandmother and smiled weakly.

Everything he'd done amounted to this—an hour-long funeral officiated by an old preacher that didn't even know what he'd looked like.

Hard to justify Eureka, looking at something like that. Wanting to live a full life, wanting to buck the harness that society put on you—that was fine. But how much was it worth? What sort of life did Geoff have?

After the funeral, I directed Nora to a nearby stream at the corner end of a public park. We sat by the water, sharing fast food she'd picked up. Everything tasted ashy and gray, like the fire ate this up too.

"I just can't stop thinking about why he didn't come out of that apartment," I said at last, after several silent minutes.

"We'll never know, I guess," Nora said.

"I wonder if he was drunk again, or high. Maybe both. I yelled, I banged on the door. How did he not hear?"

"Maybe he was a heavy sleeper," Nora said.

"How did the heat not wake him up? The smoke?"

"The fire alarms didn't go off," Nora supplied, reading back my own story to me: "Sometimes people don't wake up until it's too late. This could be that simple, Jacob. He could have suffocated in his sleep. You saved like six people, and you're a hero. Not many people would run into a burning building." She turned and looked at me. Our four feet hung over the side of a large rock, and the fast-moving water below was tumbling diamonds.

I said nothing.

Nora ran a hand over my shaved head. "I like it," she said.

"Thanks."

I faced Nora. Waves of brunette hair tossed to the side by the wind, big eyes pure pity, unadulterated compassion. The girl who would come save me even if I didn't deserve it. The girl who cared about me helplessly, who often hated the fact she did so. Indefensible love.

So I said it: "You were right. Right about Eureka. I'll quit."

Lips met mine. Nora leaned into me and she was this shaking, nervous, fragile creature in my arms, all warm concern. I fell back with her on top of me; my foot slipped into the water. Electric. Freezing cold. Every nerve ending on full alert. The sensations made me dizzy; she buried her face on my neck, lips gentle on my skin, kissing and kissing again, as though pleading with me not to change my mind. I ran a hand through her hair then leaned back, resting on the rocks with Nora in my arms.

30. The end of Eureka

I RETURNED TO SCHOOL on Monday, life still skipping by in big chunks, nothing sticking. Just a series of realizations that hours passed since the last time I realized the same thing.

Surprised by my own guilt. As events unfolded, I hadn't considered my role. Now that I stood and stared at the rubble, I wondered if I could have prevented Geoff's death and Kent's breakdown.

Could have—like, by not causing it in the first place. Did I instigate this? Cameron wasn't in love with him, and Steven pushed things too far. More than anything, Kent was delusional about his situation. So, whose fault was it?

Not such a leap to figure Steven planted the drugs in Kent's locker. I probably would have noticed if Kent was getting high; he didn't seem the type. I knew the smells, knew the slack redness of a stoner's eyes. Never saw that on Kent.

I looked at the clock again, and realized school was over. I left the building still stuck in my own head.

Cameron stopped me in the parking lot, hair aglow in the Spring sun.

"David wants us all to get together," she said. "We're having a meeting tonight."

"We are?" I asked. I hated the way everyone seemed to use 'we' to exclude me.

"Same time, same place."

"Can I get a ride?"

"Nope," she replied, turning away from me.

"Cameron!" I called to her.

"Yeah?"

"Are you okay? What's going on?"

"I'm fine," she answered. "David has been helping me through it."

The way Cameron spoke, it was clear things weren't fine—but she left before I got to ask another question.

This time, I brought a thick metal flashlight to guide my way through the woods to David's trailer. Pitch black, before I even set off. Through the narrow beam of my light, it seemed as though the forest marched across the ground toward me in a bouncing rhythm to match my own. I slipped through the bark army undetected, and found my four friends seated around a campfire, waiting.

"Hey," I said to Emily. She waved, grinning. The simple act sent my mind spinning into visions of her panting, moaning, sweating— always this way, when she was around. I forced my attention elsewhere. Didn't need Emily haunting me, not now.

Instead, I turned to Steven, searching his face for any clue he might've known what would happen with Kent. He looked smug.

David sat cross-legged in front of the charred shell of his former trailer. Pots and pans were stacked on a blanket nearby and a sleeping bag stretched out behind him, spread open and exposing its innards.

"I'm glad you're here," he said. "I called this meeting because with Kent gone, we need to determine who's 'it.'"

"That's the only reason?" I blurted. "Not to talk about if what we did was right, or wrong, or how we could make a new rule to keep this from happening again? You just want to know who's 'it' so we can keep playing without ever stopping to look back and ask what we're doing."

David's expression didn't change. "I know exactly what we're doing. Eureka only gave Kent the freedom to act. He chose what he would do. His actions resulted in a death, but Eureka is not responsible. He's in prison for who knows how long, though, and we need to figure out how the game will go on."

"Kent was a disaster. He didn't even have a good idea," Emily supplied, sucking slowly on a cigarette. "He just copied David. Kent shouldn't have been involved, ever—we're different, and you know it. The only reason he was ever invited was because Cameron kept bringing him along. Poor bastard shouldn't have been tagged in the first place."

"Geoff's dead!" I exclaimed. "How can you act like this didn't matter? Something has to change. When's the next time someone dies?"

"Kent did a stupid thing," Steven said. "It's like Emily says—he was never one of us. An outsider."

I turned to watch Cameron; she stared at the ground sullenly, hands clutching each other in her lap, thick green blanket wrapped around her shoulders. Three dead leaves from the forest floor were tangled into her hair; the blanket matched the sheet inside David's open sleeping bag.

"Kent did this because of Eureka," I said, voice rising.

"He did this because he's a dumbass," Emily countered.

"Cameron, you agree with me, right?" I asked. "You were there."

"I would think that you, of all people, would care least," Steven said. "Kent hated you, right?"

Thanks to you.

David answered before I raised a defense: "I don't know about that, Steven. If Jacob was friends with this guy who died, maybe he feels guilty."

No right answer. If I admitted to being Geoff's friend and feeling guilty, they'd say I was confused, that I wasn't at fault. But weren't we all?

I looked at Cameron helplessly, but her eyes were fixed on David.

What did I expect? They chose Eureka over a normal life, and now they couldn't have one. Hell, maybe none of us ever had a chance at being normal.

"I'm 'it,'" I claimed. "Kent tagged me after he burned down the apartment. He didn't want to play anymore. I shaved my head, for my change."

Silence.

"Excuse me for being skeptical," Steven said, "but this works out in your favor, and you *always* seem to be 'it.'"

"Cameron saw," I said.

She shifted her feet and stared into the ground for a long time. Suddenly, very shy.

"Well?" David asked. "Did you, Cameron?"

"I saw it," she said finally, into the dirt. "Jacob's telling the truth."

David nodded, and that settled the issue. "Okay then," he said. "Jacob decides who gets tagged next. But on that note, we're running out of people to play Eureka with. I think it's time we bring in some new blood, maybe even start a few more circles of players."

"You can't all be writing off this Kent disaster," I interrupted. "Because of this game, someone died—and a lot more people could have. How can that not be a serious concern? You just want to replace him? Will you do that if I die or get arrested?"

"I want the whole world to play, if it helps them. I want people to start their own rings and do this themselves. I suspect I'll need to help them, at least in the beginning. As for Kent, like I said, I don't think the game was at fault," David spoke calmly. The boy with no feelings. "The game only gives someone permission to act. Discovering how you feel can be terrifying, but the player has the responsibility and the power. That's the point. What you're feeling is survivor's guilt. Maybe you need some time to think."

"Christ," I muttered. "You're blind to it, again. You know you do this, David. You know you can't tell when you're pushing too far. I'm telling you, like I always tell you, that you need to take a step back from this and think about it. Yeah, Kent was responsible, but you pushed him into it. You're just manipulating these people. Eureka can help people, I agree, but we need to make sure people are in the right place for it."

David swept his arm across the group. "Eureka gets them ready; that's the point. Force people to accept their fears."

"Are you really trying to help people? Or just fucking with them for your amusement?" Didn't realize how much David could infuriate me. Or, always had, but never admitted it. "Look at everyone here. Are they trying to get enlightened, are they pushing themselves to deconstruct? I don't blame the game, I blame you guys. Kent was only here because he was in love with Cameron, because he wanted to impress her. Steven's got the same problem. Cameron's here because she's sleeping with you—"

"What?" The question shot from Steven's mouth.

He didn't know. Everyone was silent.

Steven rose, back stiff, still staring straight ahead, face cast orange in the fire. A log collapsed and a shower of sparks rose. Somewhere in the woods, a coyote howled, followed by the yipping of countless pups. His eyes focused, then unfocused. He looked at Cameron, then David, then back at Cameron. Finally putting it all together.

"None of that is true," Steven said, voice barely a whisper, face frozen. "I'm leaving, anyway."

David clucked his tongue and Cameron let out a distressed sigh. The group was falling apart.

Let it burn. "I'm sorry, but there has to be a line somewhere. David, you always told me I was the first person to really see what the game was. Well, I'm ending it. Someone died—that's the line."

I watched Steven; we locked eyes for a moment, preparing to walk in separate directions, away from the campfire—maybe for the last time. Steven relented first, turning and stepping off past the trees and into the forest.

"I'm not tagging any of you. Maybe never. I've been thinking about this game, what Eureka means to us, what we do with it. You guys can play without me, I don't care, but I'm not taking part. I think when the game makes us leave people we love, sometimes we lose control. Kent and Cameron—"

"You and Nora," David said.

I stumbled over my words—how much did they know about Nora? "Whatever. I don't need to hear this from you. Relationship advice from someone sitting with his harem." I turned my back on David and his madness, ready to walk away for the first time in my life.

"Wait!" Emily called out behind me. "You can't do this. Don't be a prick, Jacob! Play with us. Don't go, Jacob. I...I sort-of like you!"

I kept walking.

31. Predators circle, just past the campfire

Now

"GOOD FOR YOU," Mr. Aschen says. "I was starting to wonder if you had it in you."

"I knew you would like this part," I admit. "I don't know if what I did was right, or if I was just reacting because Geoff died and they didn't care. It did feel good to say 'no.' They left me alone for a while, too. Little bit of cold war. And what was left, anyway? Steven gone, Kent gone. David wasn't going to come beg, and I didn't know what to do. Just kept shaving my head. The weeks kept passing. Sometimes I wanted to talk to him, to tag someone, but I spent most of the time with Nora. It was going pretty good, until about last week, when things started happening. Emily things."

Last week

Hated pressing the clippers to the base of my skull. Always made me shiver, every time I ran them up my head, vibrating my brain. Shook the guilt out.

No grate, just a dank pipe down to the septic system. Staring into the drain like it was the barrel of a gun; dark hole that swallowed my mind. Never happy, even though things were going well. Had Nora. Loved Nora. But, everything suffered the effects of my own cruel conscience.

Once, I'd lectured Steven about quitting because of the people playing the game, and not the game itself. With Geoff dead, I found myself on the opposite side of my own words.

People killed people. Eureka was just a tool.

Still. I held firm, didn't tag anyone. It's all I had—hair in the drain. Penance.

Poor Geoff. Poor Kent.

No sleep. Everything disjointed, coming in staccato bits and pieces. Almost never went home—every day after school, I'd go to Nora's. Vaulted ceilings and stone floors. Where I grew up, the plastic floors gave a little bit when you put your foot down. Everything shifted and rocked with you.

Nora's home was stable. And that big window with the lake in it, and us on her couch, and we were cozy silhouettes. This was the life I never knew. Holding hands, making fun of the TV and the very stupid people who appeared on it.

Just happy to be with her. Something about her felt so *normal,* so *right.* Like things would just be easy for once.

She lived on a cul-de-sac pretty far out of town, technically another zip code. A good twenty-minute drive from the school. So, when a little blue box crept by the window at ten miles an hour, I never thought it might be coincidence.

Like everyone, I'm the subject of events out of my control. Unlike most people, my events wore oversized sunglasses and drove around in my stolen car.

Nothing to do but hold Nora closer. I didn't see Emily again, but I walked on eggshells for the rest of the night. Didn't relax until I kissed Nora goodbye outside of my dad's trailer and laid down in my cot to pretend I could ever get some sleep.

I woke up late for school and rushed to get dressed in the cramped confines of the mobile home. From sleeping to out the door in under five minutes—a skill I perfected over the years. I jogged along my usual route. It normally took me fifteen minutes to make the trek, but this time, I'd need to get there within ten or I'd miss the tardy bell and end up in detention.

I'd made plans with Nora, so that wasn't an option. These things were always a turn-off for her, and our relationship was starting to progress. I needed our time together to go smoothly for at least a few more weeks, so we could get settled down. After that, I might risk screwing up again—not that I planned on it, but these things seemed to follow me.

My old car, for instance, which was crawling up behind me and matching my jogging pace. That was bound to contain screw-ups.

I ignored her for a few moments and continued moving along. I considered running off into the trees beside the road, but didn't want to give the pale-skinned teen the satisfaction of seeing me retreat.

"Looking good," Emily called from the car.

"Leave me alone."

"We need to talk," she said.

"No, we don't. I need to get to school."

"Why?"

"What do you mean 'why?' So I can graduate."

"You never cared about that before," Emily accused.

"How do you figure?"

"I don't like yelling. Could you get in the car?"

"Not a chance in hell," I said, remembering the last time I'd been in a car with her.

"Well, can we at least stop so I can talk to you?"

"No," I said, "and stop following me."

"I need you," Emily said. "You're right about everyone else. David is not as fun anymore. Too much Cameron. And now I'm losing you, too, and it's all because of that little lame-ass Nora."

This made me stop. She stopped as well, but too slowly, and I got hit by my own car. The bumper rammed the side of my knee, knocking me onto my hands, grill inches from my face.

"Leave me alone," I said, climbing up. "You don't want to admit I could leave, because then it might make you stupid for not quitting."

"You know I can't do that," she said, grinning behind oversized shades. "This is the one thing that keeps me occupied."

"You need a hobby."

"I need Eureka. So do you. So we cracked an egg—so what?"

"Shut up," I said, voice hollow. "You have no idea. Geoff *died*, he was my friend."

"Was he? Funny, I didn't get that impression. I thought you were ashamed of him."

"Shut up," I repeated, shaking my head. "You don't get it. I doubt you can." A car approached in the distance, fog lights bouncing over potholes in the road.

"I can't...I can't be myself, Jacob. My self has problems. Look, I could play the game without you, but it wouldn't be the same. What's the point of changing all the time if no one around knows who you've been?"

The approaching car fully formed as it emerged from the morning mist. A police patrol, crowned with a rack of lights and antennas. I began waving my arms at the cruiser, trying to get his attention.

Emily noticed. She slunk low in the stolen car, pulling around me and past the cop. As the policeman passed, I stuffed my hands in my pockets and decided to walk to school. Suddenly, being on time didn't matter as much.

32. Self defense

Now

"WE HAVE DANGEROUS MINDS, Mr. Aschen. Playing Eureka made us realize certain truths about life that many people claim they understand, but don't really know like we do. We've lived through the experiments."

Mr. Aschen smirks. "Like what, Jacob?"

"Well, Steven knows that for the most part, other people decide our identity. We learned that by playing Eureka."

"You're wrong. Everyone decides who they are," he says.

"Do they? Everyone can choose how they see themselves, that's true. But they can't decide how other people see them. And which one affects you most? Let me ask you, because it's very relevant to my situation: If everyone thinks you're a murderer, but you know that you're innocent, how much does it matter? You're still in prison."

He grunts, nods. "That's an extreme example."

"Steven's an extreme guy. He knows how this works, because he knows Eureka. He started to dabble in the black arts. Dangerous weapons, Mr. Aschen."

Two days ago

The last day of school. When I arrived, Steven was waiting—perched on one of the cement banisters, next to the stairs. His hair all freshly tipped, blond spikes molded into peroxide points. Little rectangular glasses, diamond stud earring.

Steven's face was the worst. Just radiant smugness, begging someone, anyone to please punch him. Every smile, every pause—everything, Steven trying to convince everyone of his own genius. I'd witnessed the same snide superiority in the people who made fun of me for being poor. Except, Steven was poor too, and that somehow made it even more annoying. Weird, what you see in your childhood friends once you get older, get some distance.

I tried walking past without saying a word, but he called out to me: "Tag me. Tag me, and I won't do what I have planned today."

I stopped halfway up the steps and turned to face him. "You quit," I reminded him. "Why would I tag you?"

He smirked and glanced to the side before facing me again. "You quit, *I* am just starting a new group. And I want you in it. Let David hang out with the girls, I don't care. We'll have new girls."

"You don't know any girls, Steven."

"I'll meet them," he said, arms folded across his chest.

"You put weed in Kent's locker."

"I know. Interesting, right? How you can just put something in someone's possession—easy enough to do—and now their identity is changed. They are responsible for my action, which now defines them. Even if they have no idea who did it. That's powerful, you know? Interesting stuff."

"It's not happening," I said. "If I ever tag someone, it won't be you. Mostly out of spite. I don't really give a shit, Steven."

I walked past. He stood, mouth open, but said nothing.

Wished I really didn't give a shit. Unfortunately, the threat probably wasn't a joke. I didn't want to end up in jail or kicked out of school—what would Nora think?

He could've done anything. Maybe nothing—maybe his plan was to make me paranoid. If so, his plan worked.

The first two classes of the day passed without incident, which only made me more nervous. Went to my locker between first and second, checking for some hidden paraphernalia. Nothing.

Then, third period. No Cameron. Her seat was empty.

"What's wrong?" Nora asked as I sat down and froze with my hands clutching the desk, staring at an empty chair.

"I...I just don't feel good," I lied. Strange, for Cameron to miss school. There were no coincidences today.

"Go see the nurse," she said. "And I hope you feel good enough to come by tonight."

"What?"

"You've gotta listen to me rehearse my speech," she said. "You promised, remember?"

"Speech?"

"My valedictorian speech, asshole. Come on. If you go home early, give me a call and I'll pick you up after school."

"Right, right," I said. "No, I'm fine. I just need a second."

I felt flushed and frail. I wanted to explain things to Nora, but she wouldn't understand. The moment I said the word 'Eureka,' she'd get pissed.

"All right, class," the teacher said. "Today is the big day. Today, I want a picture with all my favorite graduating seniors."

The teacher was like this. Constantly reliving high school, experiencing her wonder years vicariously through us. Worried about popularity—bad enough when the kids did it.

I'd been hearing about the photo shoot for weeks, but with everything happening, I'd forgotten. From the frustrated look on Nora's face, she'd forgotten, too.

We filed out of the room and chatted our way down to the front doors of the school, where we interrupted foot traffic and took several horrible pictures with the teacher while she pretended to be best friends with all of us.

This interruption put me further on edge. I didn't want anything *unusual* happening today. After fifteen minutes of awkward hugs and high-fives, we were back inside. And here, my problems began.

"My phone!" shrieked a girl from across the classroom. "Someone stole my phone!"

"Check again," the teacher said. "Are you sure it's gone?"

"It was in my purse," she said. "I had it earlier. Someone stole it." Voice in hysterics.

Nora shrugged at me.

"Did you have the phone in *this* class?" the teacher asked.

"Yeah, just fifteen minutes ago."

"Let's look, then. Maybe it fell out of your purse."

Other students bent and twisted in their chairs, searching for something that was obviously not in plain view. The teacher was getting frustrated.

A growing knot of dread in my throat invited me to check my own backpack. I'd left it in the room while we got our pictures taken.

With a breath of resignation, I pulled my bag open. A small square of neon blue light stared back at me. A pink cell phone, resting at the bottom of my things. Next to that, a woman's white leather wallet.

The phone let out a loud chirp; the screen displayed a text message from an unknown number. The message read: *Tag me.*

I finally had a cell phone, and it was going to get me kicked out of school. I reached into the bag to turn the phone off, but the screen claimed the device was locked. I fumbled with the keys blindly for a moment, with no luck. Couldn't erase the message or shut the damn thing down without more time to fool with it.

"Jacob?" the teacher asked. I looked up from my bag to find her standing right in front of me. "Did you find something?"

"No," I said, pulling my hand out of my backpack. The room was silent, now; everyone watched me.

"Well?" the teacher asked. "I just heard a phone go off. Is that all the explanation we get?"

"It sounded like mine," she called from across the room.

"It's mine," I lied. "Sorry for having it on."

Only Nora knew me well enough to realize this was a lie. Having her around was becoming a real liability. Without her there, I wouldn't have to play by the rules. Without her, I wouldn't have to graduate. Of course, without her, nothing else would matter.

"It was his phone," Nora supplied. "I saw."

The valedictorian was unimpeachable. The teacher accepted this. She moved back to her desk at the front of the class.

Oddly attractive, finding out Nora would lie for me. After a few moments passed, I put my bag on the floor and pretended to shuffle through it. I flipped open the snap on the woman's wallet: The teacher's face on a driver's license stared back at me. Yanked my hand out—might as well have a bag full of snakes. The teacher's goddamn wallet, in my bag.

The clock laughed down at me from the wall. Still fifteen minutes left in the class. This was Steven's game. Violate my persona without my consent; forcibly shape who I am seen as. Where Eureka encouraged us to change ourselves, my rival now decided it would be better to simply force the change on other people for them. He did it to Kent, and now it was my turn.

Why didn't we have a say? What bullshit, this life. Identities were open safes anyone could tamper with, if they were willing.

"Why don't we call her phone?" some helpful little prick asked.

"That's a good idea," the teacher said, reaching into her desk drawer for her own cell phone. "What's your number?"

The girl began calling the number out. Decision time. If my backpack got searched, the teacher's wallet would be found, and I'd be in much, much bigger trouble.

"I have it," I announced. "I have her phone."

As the words left my mouth, the teacher pressed the final button on her cell phone. My backpack started singing some bullshit radio jingle.

The class tittered as I pulled the device out. "Is this your phone?" I asked the girl. Could feel Nora's disappointed stare burning holes in my back. "Uh, I found this in the hallway, on the floor by some lockers. I thought maybe it was someone else's. My other friend lost her phone, too." A lifetime of quick lies.

"You clearly knew the phone was hers," my teacher pointed out. "You confessed."

Knew I'd have to dig a little deeper. "Look, my sister just broke her front tooth on some shot and she's upset, and I thought I could give her the phone to make her feel better and..." I blubbered on, playing up my reputation as the poor trashy kid.

The teacher snatched the phone from me, which shut me up. She handed it to the girl. "Is the phone okay?"

Call a goddamn medic.

"Yeah, looks all right," the girl answered slowly, though she seemed puzzled for a moment as she cleared Steven's mysterious text from the screen.

"Do you want him to go to the office?"

I put my hands together in a praying motion and mouthed *'Please'* to the girl, whom I'd never spoken to before.

"He's a jerk," the girl said, "but it's okay. I mean, it's the last day, and I have a little sister, too."

"That's good of you, Samantha," the teacher said.

I hunched down in my seat; could feel everyone's eyes on me. Could hear the murmurs. And why? For something Steven did. Wasn't this how it always was, though? How often was someone despised in this high school for something they had no control over?

"What the hell?" Nora whispered ferociously. "You're stealing now?"

"It's not like that. I was set up," I said. And this was the worst. I could give a shit about the rest of them—but Nora mattered. Nora was real.

"Yeah, right."

"I'm serious," I whispered. "There's this guy, Steven; he's doing this to me."

Nora shook her head and turned away, silent. I could hardly blame her; this was exactly the kind of craziness I'd promised would end at Geoff's funeral.

As the bell rang for the class to end, I flew out the door. Just in time, too. As I stepped around the corner, I heard the teacher yelling for everyone to come back in. I didn't have time to check if anyone watched; as quickly as possible, I snatched the teacher's wallet from my backpack and tossed it into a nearby trashcan. The teacher rounded the corner a moment later.

"Stop right there, young man," she said, voice tinged with panic. This was the most she'd worked all year.

"Yes?" I asked.

"My wallet is missing. It was right here." She opened up her purse and demonstrated where the wallet usually sat.

"I don't have your wallet," I said.

"Don't you dare move. We're gonna put an end to your little crime spree."

Nora joined the crowd of people who gathered to see what was happening. Almost as good as a fist fight. I only prayed no one saw me throw the wallet into the garbage.

The teacher returned with a security guard, who took the backpack off my shoulders and dug around carefully, like my bag was gonna be full of needles.

I stared at Nora; she stared at the trashcan. She'd seen. Rip my heart in two. This was as bad as getting caught. She shook her head then turned away.

"Nothing," the security guard reported.

"If I find out you are responsible for this, I'm going to make sure you don't graduate," the teacher scowled.

I shrugged. "All right. That's your prerogative. Can I go to my next class now?"

The teacher didn't say anything. Just walked away.

The security guard was staring me down, so I smiled, turned, and left.

I spent the rest of the day trying to apologize to Nora between classes. By the last bell, I'd gotten her to talk to me again.

"I don't like this, Jacob."

"I know this seems crazy. Look, it's almost over. If I can graduate, I can get away from them forever."

"Who is 'them?'" Nora asked.

"The other kids from Broadway. They're...hunting me, I guess."

"I thought you quit all this."

"I did, I promise. My quitting is the reason they're doing this—I didn't steal that girl's cell phone and I definitely wouldn't steal a teacher's wallet."

"I saw you throw it away," she said as we walked through the emptying halls. "Someone should tell the teacher where her wallet is." She seemed to reconsider for a moment. "I do hate her, though."

"I'm willing to bet Steven did that. The little geeky kid? You may not remember him; he dropped out of school a year ago."

We stopped in front of my locker. The lock was gone; I swung my backpack off my shoulders and dug through the bag, yanking out my keychain. My locker key was gone, too.

This day just kept getting better. Steven must have taken my key and lock.

"What's the matter?" Nora asked.

"I'm not sure yet. Someone's been in my locker," I said, hoping to use my honesty as a preemptive defense for whatever Steven had in store. "There's gonna be something messed up in here. Maybe drugs. A human head? The way this day is going, maybe a fist will fly out and hit me in the face. I have no idea, Nora. I think he's trying to prove something to me, like he's the smartest guy on Earth. Over-compensating, if you ask me."

"Your life is freaking ridiculous. You know that, right?" she asked, thick brown eyebrows furrowed.

I opened the locker. Inside, a note. On it, one word: *Boo.*

I blushed. "Like I said. He's out to get me."

Nora rolled her eyes. "Look, I'm trying to trust you."

"Seriously?" I shoved the note into the back of the locker, putting my books over the paper. "I thought you'd get pissed and leave, honestly."

She shrugged. "I don't think many people have trusted you before. You might not be used to this. No offense, but you don't inspire confidence."

"I just wish these people would leave me alone." That was partially true. Sort of.

"What exactly does Steven want?" Nora asked.

"He wants to be better than David, and I'm the only person who knows them both. I'm the only one who can justify him. They're kind of in a contest to see who's craziest."

"And is he really better? I mean, crazier?" Nora asked.

"No, not nearly."

"*You* aren't going to start acting crazy again, are you? I don't know if I can handle that." Worry warped the deep wells of her eyes.

"I'm not, okay? Let's go to your house. I'll listen to your speech. I'm sure you'll do great." Changing the subject to tomorrow's festivities seemed to lighten the mood.

"I'm so nervous," she admitted. "I have to give a speech to the entire school. You remember when David did his last year?"

I remembered all too well. "I don't think you'll top that for entertainment value."

33. The weapon of choice

Now

"FRAMING. It's an interesting thing to call it, don't you think? Putting someone in a particular view."

Mr. Ashen answers me: "But, Nora trusted you. Her view of you didn't change when you got framed. Doesn't that mean anything to you?"

Maybe it does. Maybe my problem is, no one loved me up until that moment. Still, that doesn't help what happened next.

"That kind of trust has limits, Mr. Aschen. Those limits got tested that very same day—tested and broken."

———— ✶ ————

Two days ago

Just me and Nora, unsupervised in her house. Finally, some sanctuary. Nothing could touch us in that nice, clean home with a church ceiling and stone floors that made the greatest sound when my shoe struck them. The sound of civilization.

No wasting the hour between when we got to her place, and her father got off work. We quickly became a heap of writhing clothes on her bed. Nora's hot breath tickled the stubble on my face, and my hands found their way into the wonderfully warm space between her blouse and skin.

She stopped kissing me as I worked to undo her bra. "You were weird today. None of that for you."

"Oh, c'mon. Being a little weird never hurt anyone."

She became rigid and pushed me away, and I knew I'd said something wrong. "Sometimes when you get weird—it ends up hurting me in the process. Do you really think 'being weird' is in your best interest at this point?"

"I don't think I have any idea what 'normal' is, I'm trying—"

Nora screamed—not at me, but in genuine fear.

I twisted under her, turning to follow her horrified stare.

Emily waved at us through Nora's window, face inches from the glass. "Hey, guys," she said loudly. The cheeriness in her voice was muffled by the pane between us.

What the hell. Emily, here. Why? Could be any reason; Emily was crazy. I froze in the face of all the different ways this could go. Did she have a weapon? No. Was she breaking in? Not yet.

"What's *she* doing here?" Nora asked, climbing stiffly from her position on top of me.

I understood only the basics. "Emily plays Eureka. She wants me to tag her," I answered.

"You mean after I saw this skank kissing you, you still have *anything* to do with her?" Nora asked, loudly enough for Emily to hear. "I thought it was pretty well assumed that if we were a couple, you wouldn't be hanging out with any exes."

She stood patiently outside, arms crossed behind her back, until we'd finished. "Can I come in?" Emily asked. "It's hot out here."

"No," I said. "Look, I wouldn't touch her."

"Except that one time," Emily supplied helpfully.

"You dick," Nora said, punching me in the shoulder.

"I thought you hated me. And it was for Eureka..."

"Eureka and orgasms. If you could—" Emily tried to say.

"What is she talking about?"

"This was before you came and picked me up on Christmas." I said, trying to calm Nora. "When we weren't talking."

"Proceed to the front door..." Emily continued, folding her arms.

"I'm trying to explain. Look," I put a hand on Nora's shoulder, which she flung off.

"YELLOW SKITTLES!" Emily shouted, finally getting our attention. We both turned and looked at her. "They're my favorite out of the bunch."

"What the hell are you talking about?" I asked.

"Let me in, kiddies," Emily said. "We can sit down and talk like grownups. Or, alternatively, Jacob can tag me and I will go home."

"You've always been a total bitch to me," Nora said. "Why would you come to my house? How do you even know where I live?"

"I thought your calming influence might help me talk some sense into Jacob," Emily said.

I rubbed a hand across my face in frustration. Her presence alone had nearly broken us up. Had to get Emily out of here, fast—but what could I do? I wasn't ready to give up.

"I will give your car back, Jacob," she said, dangling my keys at me. "I'm tired of running from the police, anyway. Just tag me, goddamnit."

"You can have the car," I said.

"Wait—why does she have your car?" Nora asked.

"He gave it to me," Emily said. I scowled at her. "Let me in, and I'll tell you all about it. I've got tons of dirty secrets."

"There is no way are you coming in!" Nora said, arms crossed, lips pressed tightly together.

"I didn't give her the car—Eureka made me," I tried to explain.

"How can a game make you do something? Why didn't you tell the cops?" Nora asked.

"I couldn't. It would have been..." I struggled to think of the words.

"Poor sportsmanship?" Emily supplied, her voice still muffled.

"Sorta," I agreed.

"Let's move this to the front, so I can kick you both out," Nora quietly decided, shaking her head. "I cannot handle this right now. Jacob, I'm trying. I really am. You're making this too hard."

As we walked through the house to the front door, I tried to reason with her. She wasn't having it. Nora shut down, and my words fell on deaf ears.

Emily waited outside, one arm up against the side of the home, the other one holding a cigarette to her lips. Short maroon dress pushed against her curves by the wind, night to the day of Nora's blue jeans and t-shirts.

"Put that out," Nora demanded. "You'll make the whole place stink."

Emily ignored her. "Jacob, if you tag me, I'll leave," she said. "I don't mean to break your life. I only want what I want. I want what we had."

Tagging her was tempting, I had to admit. Every moment she spent here, she destroyed the weeks I'd spent rebuilding trust with Nora.

She continued: "We had a good thing going, Jacob. Let's start it again. Just tag me, promise me, and then you can go back to banging the nerd, all right?"

"Hey," Nora objected.

I didn't know how to defend a girl from another girl.

Emily addressed Nora next. "He is in a state of denial. I know that he knows Eureka is a beautiful thing. I've seen it in him. Except, now he's got a girlfriend, and he's scared to lose her, so he's changing. He's changing by refusing to change. You're ruining him."

Nora turned to me. "Would you get this crazy bitch off my lawn?"

"What am I supposed to do, drag her by the hair?"

"It would be a nice start," Nora said. Emily stared. "Just get her out of here. I can't handle this." Tears sprung up in the corners of her eyes. "What do you two want from me?"

I put my arms around Nora and hugged. She held her hands up so all I felt were elbows and forearms.

Emily spoke again: "Jesus, she's got a fragile mind. It's not that —"

She was interrupted as Nora shoved me back and away from her, turned, and punched Emily in the mouth. Her fist connected with a solid *thwack* and my temptress stumbled backward in her platform shoes, falling onto the soft grass, cigarette landing several feet away.

"You *punched* me," Emily said in shock, wiping her mouth with her forearm.

"You should go," I said. "She's probably going to do it again."

Nora was sniffing back tears. She spun around, shoved me away from the door, and slammed it between us.

"Nora, come on. I didn't do this!"

"Go to hell, both of you!" I heard her cry.

"Son of a bitch," I proclaimed to no one in particular.

Emily was still on the ground behind me. She extended a hand so I could help her up. "Not this time," I said, walking past.

34. The Grackle King

THE ROAD OUT OF NORA'S NEIGHBORHOOD cut through fields of corn which stood golden brown and six feet high. As I walked, my legs seemed to power the gears in my mind, which struggled to grind through this last chunk of experience.

Emily was right. Would I stay with Nora? Was Nora even an option, after what Emily did?

Hot May sun baking me, radiating my skin. They say in a billion years, the sun will devour the Earth. Texas is the appetizer. Three hours of walking to do, but at least dusk would set in before long.

I heard a car slowing down behind me, but I didn't bother turning my head. Figured I knew who it was.

"Go away," I said as the window rolled down with a squeak. "You've done enough. I'm still not tagging you."

"Just wanted to give you a lift, Jacob," David said. "That's what friends do, right?"

I turned, shocked. David sat in a beat-up red sports car with a mismatched hood and door. His arm relaxed out the window, sleeves of his flannel shirt rolled up to the elbows. A constant grumble emanated from the car's hood, punctuated by a few odd bursts of noise. "This yours?" I asked, secretly relieved to see him.

"Someone loaned it to me. Sort of."

I walked around to the passenger side. "How've you been?"

"I've been tired," David said, and he looked it. Deep lines of worry radiated from the pits of his eyes, as though the orbs smashed into his face at great speed and left cratered Earth behind.

"You look like shit," I commented.

"You look even worse. How've you been?"

"I'm alive," I said. "That's enough, right?"

"Sometimes just waking up in the morning is a victory," David said, putting the car in drive, easing up to speed on the farm road as loose stones kicked up into the undercarriage.

We didn't speak for the first five minutes. I think he wanted me to talk first—but I wasn't sure what to say. After a while, he seemed to relent. "I thought you'd come back by now. I'm surprised, Jacob, and a little disappointed."

I rested my chin on my hand, staring out the open window. "I've been a little bit of an idiot," I said. "Emily was just explaining it to me, actually."

He grinned. "Oh yeah?"

We reached the edge of Kingwood forest; it sped past us. Called to mind riding stolen bikes down this same road all those years ago. "I love Eureka. It's the opposite of modern life, and at the same time, it's exactly what our lives are, if we're willing to admit we don't really have control. But, something happened to the group. I can't go back, not to you and Cameron and Steven. We ruin each other."

"You still want to quit?" he asked. The pain in his voice was evident, and it cut at my chest. "What if I make some changes? What if I promise to really listen to you?"

"Do you really care what I think? I wonder, sometimes. Aren't you just going to do what you do, no matter what I say?"

"I'm not, now," David answered. "I haven't been for a few weeks. Been waiting on you, honestly."

"I don't believe that," I said. "But if you do care what I think, then yes. What if Eureka is a great idea, but we as human beings are totally screwed? Aren't some ideas like that? You know, they sound good on paper, but when you try to make it work, you find out the people involved ruin it. Steven and Kent only wanted to use Eureka to make other people do what they want them to do. Emily, Cameron and me—okay, great. We can play the game the right way. Except, you're sleeping with Emily *and* Cameron. So where am I supposed to fit in? And, David—someone died, you know? Because Kent thought Eureka could make Cameron like him, or that it could erase his past and his dad's past."

David sighed heavily. "Maybe you're right. Maybe this was a mistake. I think I'm doing the right thing, but, sometimes I don't feel like I can tell. I look at the people around me, and... am I hurting them?"

"You're pushing them," I said. "Sometimes they break. You need to develop your own sense of right and wrong. Or, you need to accept that concepts like *right* and *wrong* do apply, even to you. Maybe you are responsible for some suffering, for some failures. Maybe a part of Geoff's death is your fault—and my fault, too. Can you accept that?"

David looked like he was about to say something, but never did. Almond eyes squinted behind brown curls, as beautiful a creature as ever. We arrived back at Broadway. Grackles fluttered, harkening the arrival of their king with a confetti blast of loose feathers.

The car rolled to a halt. "I'm starting to worry I ruined everything," he said, voice low.

"It's not so bad," I told him. "You'll bounce back from this. You're a genius, David. Whatever you do next will be even better; you just needed to learn, first. Here, I've got something that might cheer you up." I put a hand on his shoulder. "Tag. I may not want to be your conscience anymore, but I still want to see you do amazing things."

I stepped out of the car, leaving David to his thoughts. I couldn't stand to see him sounding depressed or lost; it was so out of character. Tore my heart out.

"Thanks, Jacob," David's voice carried through the passenger side window as it rolled down. "You've been a good friend. The best."

35. I blame the death of David Bloom on...

Yesterday

I TRIED CALLING NORA THAT NIGHT. She didn't answer, so I left a message on her machine: "I feel awful about what happened. Look, there are no excuses. What I did was stupid. Without you, Eureka is the one thing I have that makes me special. You're right, though—when I play, you get hurt. I'm sure you will do fine at graduation tomorrow. I'm sorry I didn't get to hear you practice your speech yesterday. I'm sure it's great. I love you."

Felt a little better after that, but I still mined up deep veins of self-pity every time I let my mind wander. I told myself things would be better for Nora if I wasn't around; she didn't need me in her life. Separating was for the best.

I went to sleep feeling as depressed and lost as I ever had.

Sound and fury woke me at four in the morning. I rolled over and peered out my small window in time to see a car colliding with Mr. Gimble's trailer. Mass smashing mass, chassis splitting chassis in rapid action, gas splashing. Maniacal music of plate glass crashing, plastic cracking, both vehicles splitting apart, axles clashing. The car's remaining headlight rolled to a stop against a tree near the landlord's abandoned trailer. I jumped out of bed and was out the door in moments, running over the wet grass in bare feet to the car, to see if anyone was injured.

Except, that was *my car*. The little blue box didn't deserve this: used as a weapon against Mr. Gimble's property, blue aluminum exterior peeled back like soda cans after target practice. I dashed around to the other side, jumping over the detached bumper, but found no sign of life. The door was open and I searched the area, peering into the darkness. No trace of Emily or anyone else.

No one inside the car, either, except for a pack of cigarettes on the floorboard of the driver's side. I took them, wondering if they were Emily's. One cig remained, with familiar handwriting on the side. *Hell is other people.*

"What the hell did you do?" Dad's voice was a brutal growl.

"Nothing. I was asleep, I just ran out here."

His eyes narrowed, arms folded, posture screaming disbelief.

"Seriously!" I demanded. "Look at my clothes, I don't even have shoes on. Besides, I haven't seen this car in months."

"You're lying, somehow," he said. "I'm gonna call the police and report this. But I know you're lying somehow. You told me this got stolen. Who is gonna steal a car then drive it back to the owner's property? You're guilty somehow."

Well, partially true. I looked at Mr. Gimble's abandoned trailer. The window where he'd written his selling price and phone number was smashed. A microwave had flown out, open and dirty with burnt-on sauces, cord dangling uselessly on the lawn—little box refrigerator, toaster, shelf full of silverware spread out on the grass.

Dad put his hands on either side of the car's mangled frame and leaned into the open door. "Look at this shit!" he exclaimed, pulling the shattered remains of a liquor bottle from the car. "Are you drunk?"

I stared at him, exasperated. "Do I look drunk, Dad? It's four in the morning. I was sleeping like five feet away from you all night."

He stood next to me. The two of us stared at the ravaged trailer. A pool of fluid bled onto the soil; I stepped back to keep it from getting on my feet.

"Least it hit the right trailer," I said.

"You shut up," Dad scolded, anger lacing his voice. "I know you had something to do with this, and I don't want to hear you making light of it."

"Whatever," I mumbled.

"What'd you say?" he threatened.

I ignored him, walking back to the trailer and getting dressed to the sound of policemen and tow trucks. By now, most of our neighbors had formed a circle around the scene of the accident, sipping coffee and speculating as to what happened.

While I was inside, the phone rang. I answered.

"Hello?"

"Hello, Jacob." Steven's voice.

"You did this," I said immediately.

"Emily is surprisingly easy to steal from. But that's beside the point: It looks like *you* did this. How are you gonna explain how *your* stolen car ended up crashed into *your* neighbor's trailer?" Steven asked.

"You're insane. What if you killed someone?"

"I'm not stupid. I knew that place was empty. Just aim it, jam a stick between the gas and dash, not rocket science. I mean, we're all about changing identities, right? Well, let's see how you like these changes. Jacob Thorke: felon."

"You're full of shit," I said. "Get this over with and get to the point. I'm so sick of you trying to impress me with these games. This is not what Eureka is about; I'm not tagging you, and I'm not playing Eureka with you. Let it rest."

"This is the best way to play, Jacob. Eureka doesn't make people friends; we've been doing it wrong. Competition, challenging each other, that's what builds character. That's what gets you out of your shell. Look, you don't have to answer now. Today, at ten—come to the water tower instead of graduation. I'll be waiting."

"I tagged David yesterday. You're on your own, Steven—" He hung up; my words fought over airspace with a dial tone. I slammed down the receiver, pissed, trying to decide if I should actually go to the water tower.

I looked at the cap and gown wadded up on my bed. Limp things, meaningless pomp. And going to graduation meant watching Nora give her speech. I tried to have it all, and now I had nothing. I picked up the black robe and tossed it into the trash.

Dad banged on the side of the trailer, yelling for me to get out. I did, and he waved me over to a uniformed cop with a notepad. A dark tattoo of a Chinese symbol barely registered over the blackness of his forearm. "You know anything about this? Your dad says this car was yours when it got stolen," the policeman asked, swatting at a moth which fluttered in the glow of his headlight.

I told him the same story I gave my father. "The car got stolen months ago. I don't know why it's here."

"You know who stole this car in the first place?"

"We filed a report. Some girl who called herself 'Moira Blocker' scammed me. We were supposed to meet for sex and she took my car." Pretty much the truth, right? "You guys know everything I know. Look, I'm graduating from high school today. I want to get some sleep. Do you think I finally got my car back, then I wrecked it? Can I please go?"

The officer's eyes narrowed. "I want him to take a Breathalyzer." The statement wasn't made to me, but to my father. He nodded.

"Sure, whatever," I shrugged. "Better let me leave if I pass."

"Kids don't tell me what I better or better not do. Now, take a deep breath. All right, blow out into this little tube."

He held a plastic device up to my mouth, and I exhaled slowly. When I was finished, he studied the device with squinted eyes, angling it into his headlights to see.

"All right," he said. "No alcohol. Don't go anywhere, though. I know you don't have a car to run with." He put the pen and pad into his shirt pocket. "You know if the owner of that trailer had any enemies?"

I laughed, despite myself. "Ask any of the neighbors, they can fill you in. But yeah, he had enemies: everyone, even the birds."

In the end, who was I kidding? I had to see what Steven planned. Even if I just watched, I needed to know what he was doing. I learned the hard way that ignoring him didn't solve anything.

I rode my bike up to the water tower. Got there about ten, when Steven said to meet. I didn't go all the way up to the tower, though, because I figured he probably had some stupid elaborate plan, and I didn't want to walk right into it. So I held back about a hundred feet, just looking. Didn't see anything. Stayed another ten minutes, and still didn't see anything.

Then, when I was just about to give up and go home, I saw something at the edge of the water tower, up top. Two shapes. One of them fell. Never seen anything like it; felt like I was the one falling. And the *sound*—I heard it. The worst sound in the world. I started running up to the tower, and the closer I got, the more it looked like David. Then I saw someone else coming down the water tower ladder, but he had a mask on. For some stupid reason, I thought David might be need help, so I didn't chase him." I stopped and cleared my throat. "But he was dead, of course."

Universes collided as Mr. Aschen leans in.

"Who was it, Jacob?"

"What do you think?"

The color drains from Mr. Aschen's face. "Steven. It fits, I think. Are you sure that's who you saw?"

"Like I said, he had on a mask. But, he was the right size. The right build. And he told me to meet him at the water tower. Who else knew to be there?"

"And you think he drove your car into Mr. Gimble's trailer in an attempt to frame you?"

"He called me and took credit, that's all I can say for sure. But since you asked me, here's what I think happened: Steven wanted to be David, but that position was already filled. So, Steven wanted to take Eureka and start over on his own. That would be this big victory for him, to take the game away from David and then start his own group. Maybe take credit for the whole idea. First, he tried to convince me to tag him with that debacle in History class. Then, maybe he knew about Emily coming to Nora's and figured I'd tagged her; when he found out she wasn't 'it' either, he took her car and came back for me. That morning, after he wrecked the car, I talked to him on the phone and told him David had the tag. I think he went after David next, and that's when things got out of control. Or, maybe he already knew David was 'it,' and he only wanted me at the water tower so he could frame me for murder."

Mr. Aschen leans back, left hand clutching his jaw, as though he must hold his mouth in place. "If you suspected Steven, why didn't you just tell me?"

"I don't have any proof. If I just told you, it wouldn't mean anything. Besides, I may be angry at Steven, Mr. Aschen, but I don't want him to go to prison. At least, not unless he really murdered David."

The door to the interview room flies open. A familiar face appears: the detective. In his hands, a plastic grocery bag—can't tell what's inside. He enters the room fully and closes the door behind him, then leans down until he's inches from my nose.

He reaches into the plastic grocery sack and retrieves a smaller sandwich bag with a single, half-smoked cigarette inside. "This look familiar?" the detective asks, sour breath hot on my cheeks, the smell of bismuth syrup and hot sauce.

"Can't say it does. I don't smoke. What's that written on the cigarette? 'Hell is?'"

He presents the second plastic bag and the identically branded pack of cigarettes within. "Same writing on all these. Little messages. One of them says 'Hell is other people.' You sure these don't look familiar?"

I look up at him, lock eyes, summon every ounce of earnestness. "I don't smoke, officer. I've never seen them."

"If you're lying to us, then we'll find that out, too."

"That's fine," I say. "I'm broke, officer. I don't smoke."

The detective sighs.

My counselor's legs are crossed and clenching each other tightly, as though this is the only way he can keep from jumping up. "I believe Jacob, for what it's worth."

"Not much," the detective says.

Mr. Aschen lifts his hands, as if to say *what now?*

"Listen," the detective addresses me as he scratches his scalp. "Don't think about leaving Kingwood. Just because I'm not arresting you today, doesn't mean this is over. We've got Steven here now, and if his story conflicts with yours, you'll be back here."

"Then I don't have anything to worry about," I say. "Because I didn't kill David."

The detective grunts. "We'll see. For now, our focus has shifted. I'll have someone escort you out. Thanks for your stay; I hope you found the accommodations hospitable."

I shake my head, dazed from a lack of sleep and the events of the day—too confused and conflicted to make sense of it all. I'm let out of the room then led through the maze that is the police station. Someone hands me my shoes and wallet.

I end up on the front steps, wondering what the hell is next for me. I don't have to wonder long—the one person who cannot deny me, much like I couldn't deny David, is here waiting.

Nora's car is parked on the street, and she's leaning against it.

"Hey," I say, walking up to her. "Didn't expect to see you here."

"I could turn around," she offers. "Turn around and go home."

"Please don't."

"Maybe I should." She's angry, I can tell. That's a good thing; if she's angry, there's still hope. "You missed graduation. I rocked the speech."

"I heard the whole thing. I was a few hundred yards away, with David. I mean, David's body."

"I heard. What happened?"

"No idea," I say. "They think Steven did it. Don't know why."

Nora clucks her tongue and opens her door. "Are you okay?" she asks. "Weren't you and David friends?"

"When we were kids. This has been weird, yeah. I need to sleep. I'll be all right eventually, though. They questioned me all night."

She looks concerned for a moment, then recovers her stern frown.

I open the passenger door; we crouch into her car and she begins driving away from the police station.

"And all this—I mean, David dying—this has nothing to do with Emily coming over?" she asks. "With history class and the stolen wallet?"

"Absolutely nothing," I lie.

"You're lying. I want you to open up to me, Jacob," Nora says as she drives toward Broadway.

"Let me sleep. Then I'll tell you everything. Please, I promise. I just spent like thirty hours in an interrogation room. Did you ever get Emily off your lawn?" I ask.

"It took a while. We actually sat down and talked for a few minutes."

"Oh, really?" I'm afraid of the outcome.

"She made me think about giving you another chance. This was her fault, wasn't it? Not yours? The car being stolen, and all that?"

"We're equally guilty. She's a little crazy."

"I'll say," Nora agrees. She seems satisfied with this; maybe she's getting used to the fact my life isn't going to be normal. I can only hope. I'm tired of lying.

Done a lot of it today. Bold lies, crafted with purpose. Lies bundled in truth. Didn't want to underestimate Mr. Aschen and the detective, like I'm sure Steven will. I don't have his ego.

The first lie? Steven didn't invite me to the water tower at ten that morning; David did.

I lift up off the seat and pull my wallet from its place in my back pocket. Hidden deep within the furthest recess, in a compartment closed to unfamiliar eyes, is a sheet of paper folded into neat squares. I pull the white slip from its place. I'm lucky the police hadn't noticed this, or didn't know what it signified. Can't bear to let the note go.

There's only one word and a signature on the page.

Eureka.
-David Bloom

The grim epitaph was pinned to his chest. A final, private message to the Six.

I met him at the watchtower yesterday. I saw him fall. Not from the ground, but from ten stories in the sky. I was up there with him.

The blue bars of the narrow ladder were rough under my hands; I death gripped each rung, taking deep breaths to steady myself as I climbed up after David. When I stopped to look down, I had a feeling like the whole world spun, like I was crawling along upside down. I wrapped my right arm around the bar so I couldn't fall, held on and looked straight up until the spinning passed.

My heart pumped ice water. Microphone feedback from the graduation's PA system whined behind me. A line of black clouds stood guard of the horizon; chill tinged the edge of the breeze.

At last I reached the peak; my fingers clutched the rusty aluminum railing that lined the outer rim of the tower. Blue paint flaked away under my hands. Panic rose, beginning with a tremor in my legs and working up to my fingertips. A few more deep breaths steadied me. Hundreds of feet in the air with no railing, no safety if I tripped. A straight fall to the ground.

David stood near the far edge of the platform. Just the two of us, facing each other ten feet below heaven. His arms were outspread, fingertips extended, like he was grabbing handfuls of the wind.

There were only inches between his feet and the edge of the tower. I knew immediately that he planned to jump.

I watched the wind whip brown hair around an exhausted face, eyes squinting into the force of the gale that wailed around us. "You don't have to do this. Things can change," I yelled, words ripped to shreds as they fought through the wind dividing us.

"You were right. About Kent, about the girls, about everything. I started this experiment, and it was a stupid thing to do, but I wanted to prove I could. For whatever reason, you guys follow me. And I abused you, and I fucked everyone's lives up. I've done more; things you've never heard about. And it's all right, Jacob. I don't feel anything, I don't mind being dead. It's better than hurting people. This is the only thing I can do to try and make things right. I can take this tag to the grave with me. Goodbye, Jacob."

My friend took a small step backward toward the end of the water tower, then hobbled into another, then spun his arms as the final stumble sent him careening over the smooth edge of the construct.

I blame the death of David Bloom on myself.

All I could do was stand there in disbelief; I didn't have the courage to run to him. Instead, I just pretended he'd looked good dying.

If I was a good me, I might have told him he was full of himself, that Eureka was bigger than him, that we might play anyway.

But, I'm not a good me. We've established that. Besides, those words would have hurt him even more. Had to be all David, or none at all.

So, I haven't been perfectly honest with Mr. Aschen. Steven hadn't been at the tower, only David and I. The rest has been true, though. One tiny fabrication—a conclusion I let Mr. Aschen come to on his own.

I am the one who planted Steven's cigarette. The pack that the detective has now—those are Steven's brand, and the messages are in his handwriting. It will put him at the scene. Let him be interrogated; make him sweat a little bit. He'll lie, try to manipulate them, and maybe even wind up in prison.

Someone needs to teach Steven how a framing is supposed to work. And if anyone is guilty, anyone other than myself, he pushed David the furthest. He transformed David's life into something that couldn't be walked away from.

I made sure to be arrested; I had to act first. Steven has framed me twice already, and he'll twist David's death into something cheap. I mean, Mr. Aschen is right. I can't let people walk all over me anymore: gotta learn to say 'no' some time.

The streets of Kingwood are wet. I can only hope the rain washed away my fingerprints on the ladder rungs. If not, I always have the suicide note as a trump card. I can always tell them the truth.

I'd just rather not.

Kingwood rolls by; Nora turns onto the familiar slick, black road leading to Broadway. Grackles line it, watching us with interest, respectfully silent for once.

Thing is, telling my story to the detective, talking with Mr. Aschen like that—it does clarify things for me. Really puts my life into perspective, but probably not the way my counselor wants.

Even after all this, I'm not sure Eureka is a bad idea. *Some* good has come from Eureka. More good can come. But, can we handle it?

Nora brings the car to a stop at the trailer. I get out and walk around to her window to say goodbye. Against all hope, I lean in to kiss her. She slaps me lightly across the cheek. "Yeah, right," she says. "I'm still pissed at you. It'll be a while."

"Fair enough. I'll see you, though."

"We need to get you into college," she tells me. "Give me a call in a few days, when I'm done punching things that have your picture on them. We'll work on your finances."

"We've gotta have a long talk about that," I say, realizing I don't actually want to go. I figure, as long as I have the chance of a fresh, truthful start with Nora, I might as well go all out.

"We'll see," Nora replies. She hits the gas; the front wheels spin on the gravel for a moment before she's carried away.

I watch her car meander over the makeshift dirt roads of the trailer park. I turn; my eyes scan the dilapidated set of RVs, a graveyard of slain metal monsters and the secrets they hold. All is silent. The big dogs are sleeping in their makeshift fences and the high drama has at last turned down.

Then, somewhere in the distance—the sound of glass breaking, a cursing man, a screaming baby. Grackles burst from a tree in unison, synchronized madness. So it goes. If you squint your eyes just right, it even starts to make a little sense.

If I'm going to keep playing, I'll need people to play with. That instruction manual David wanted to write, you know? That might work, if everyone knows what to expect. If I can teach people not to make the same mistakes as Kent and Steven.

Or, maybe not. Maybe, let it all rest.

But, in the strictest sense, I can't leave Eureka, even if I try. There will always be an Emily.

Emily will come for me in one form or another. She'll come for everyone. Whether or not this is done *personally*, rest assured:

everyone will meet their Emily. She might have the face of a fire, flood, tumor or drunk driver—but she'll be there, and she'll change everything. What people call their own, they're only stealing, and Emily is coming to take it back.

Eureka or not, that's life. Throw off your burdens and revel in the chase, or live with shackled legs so chaos can stalk you with a smile on her face. It makes no difference. Change, or be changed.

Tag, you're it.

24920019R00116

Printed in Great Britain
by Amazon